ALWAYS SECOND BEST

A Broken Dreams

Novel

By
Elodie Nowodazkij

Come talk to me in my Facebook Group, Elodie's
Cozy Nook (exclusive excerpts, giveaways, group
discussion and more…)
Do you want to be entered in a **giveaway** every month
to win a free book? Sign up for my newsletter!

All information here: www.elodienowodazkij.com

ALWAYS SECOND BEST

Copyright © 2015 by Elodie Nowodazkij

For information, contact elodie@elodienowodazkij.com or visit: www.elodienowodazkij.com

Book and Cover design by Elodie Nowodazkij

First Edition: October 2015

DEDICATION

This book is for my parents, my sisters, nieces,
nephew, cousins, aunts and uncles and grandmothers,
and grandfather, for my entire family…
One says we cannot choose our families, but I would
choose you. Always.

And for my husband: we chose each other and I'm
grateful that we decide to choose each other again and
again. I love you.

CHAPTER 1 – EM

I SHOULD HAVE STAYED at the School of Performing Arts this weekend. I should have spent more time rehearsing for our big end-of-the-year showcase audition. I should have repeated each movement until I reached perfection…

I'm never going to be ready.

My throat tightens. I need more hours, more days, more time.

"Do you want more lasagna?" my grandmother—Nonna—asks. Her gray hair is cut short and even though the lines on her face are getting more pronounced, even though she's pale and thinner, even though she gets tired more easily, her smile is still the brightest in all of New York. "Or maybe more salad?" She mixes the tomato mozzarella salad again. She grows the basil herself, and believes that she could have an entire menu using only recipes with basil, like pesto steaks, or basil sorbet.

"A bit more salad, please." I hand her my plate. Nonna's restaurant is usually bright and full of laughter and people and waiters trying not to run into one another, but tonight it's only her and me. Nonna opens the restaurant for lunch on Sundays and keeps her evening free.

"There you go." She sips her water. "Your father was so cute when he was little. That day he brought me a bouquet with roses from our garden, I didn't have the heart to tell him he shouldn't have cut them. Instead, I made sure to put one in his baby book," she says and then inhales deeply as if trying to catch her breath. She smooths the red tablecloth on our small table. She called tonight a "grandmother-granddaughter" date night, setting up candles and even putting some Italian music on in the background.

Even though I should be rehearsing, I couldn't say no to her. I didn't want to say no. And not because her lasagna is the best in town.

"I'm talking, I'm talking but I know you have to go," she says, standing up, holding on to her chair.

"I can stay," I reply.

"You're sweet, but you've started to fidget on your chair, that means you're already running late."

I cringe—I hadn't noticed I was doing that. "Dinner was really delicious. Thank you." I gather the plates, but she takes them away from me.

"I'll take care of that. You go."

And there's so much tenderness in the way she looks at me that I want to bottle up the emotion I feel and keep it for when I have a bad day, or for when I see Nick—my forever crush, my brother's best friend, the guy who broke my heart last summer. I hold her arm and together we walk to the entrance. The restaurant smells of fresh bread mixed with garlic and basil. It smells of my childhood spent in the kitchen with her and Poppa.

When everything was so much easier.

I grab my coat, careful not to knock one of the pictures she has on the walls. Her memory wall, as she calls it. Lots of pictures of Poppa, and my own father, and my entire family, and of Italy. She recently put one up of Mr. Edwards, the man who has been courting her for almost a year now.

"Goodbye, Bellisima," she says, kissing my cheeks loudly. "Thanks for spending time with your old grandmother." She winks.

"You're not old."

"You're right. I'm ancient." She laughs and hugs me again. The perfume Mom gets her every Christmas is another reminder of all the happy times I've had with her. She coughs and leans against the wall. "I know you wanted to stay at school this weekend, so thank you again." And before I can reply, she pushes me out the door. "Now, go. You don't want to be late."

"Love you," I tell her. I put on my coat and my scarf.

"I love you too, Bellisima." She pauses. "And say hi to Nicholas for me," she says.

Nicholas. Nick. I force my lips into a smile, I force myself to not think about Nick. I force myself to wave to Nonna. "I'll see you next week."

And I glance at her one more time before slowly making my way to the subway. I used to love going back to school on Sundays. I used to wait for

Nick at the corner of our street and we'd walk together. We'd talk about our weekend. He'd make me laugh and I'd try to not stare at his lips while he talked about his parents, our last audition, the video game he managed to get his hands on before its release, because he knew I wanted to play it and he knew some guy who could make it happen.

That was before.

Now, I take the subway from Brooklyn, where my family and I moved after Nick's father fired my dad.

Alone.

Now, I don't spend every possible second with Nick, I don't send him random text messages to make him laugh, I don't smile every time I see him.

Now, I avoid him as much as possible and lie to his face about dating some guy I met at my Nonna's restaurant.

I readjust my bag on my shoulder and look up at the gray sky. New York has had its share of snow and winter and icy sidewalks but it seems we're in for another round, even though we're already in March. There's a small coffee shop nestled between bigger buildings one block before the subway. It's crowded and I'm tempted to push the door and get in line. Hide in there and forget about real life. Forget about school.

But instead of entering the coffee shop, I march straight ahead. I pass a group of students who are talking about an epic party they went to yesterday, and I barely avoid a couple whose PDA is so over the top I can almost hear my brother telling them to get a room. I settle in an empty seat in the subway.

ALWAYS SECOND BEST

And my mind wanders to the same game it always plays. If the third person to enter the car is a woman, I'm going to talk to Nick. Really talk to him. I'll come clean about not seeing anyone.

The first person who enters the subway is a woman with hair to her shoulders and a big smile that shows a gap in her middle teeth, and she's holding the hand of another woman with dark hair, who's the second person to enter the car. She gives her girlfriend a kiss on the lips, before whispering something into her ear. They both start giggling. The third person to enter the car is a guy. The guy's not wearing a coat despite the freezing temperatures. His Hugo Boss shirt is tight around his muscles and his jeans must cost more than an entire semester at the School of Performing Arts. Based on the price of his outfit, he's not jacketless because he can't afford one; it's a fashion statement. A fashion statement that could freeze him to death.

Maybe I could count the couple as only one person and if the next passenger is a woman, then I would talk to Nick. A group of guys enter the subway.

I sink into my seat.

The universe has spoken—I won't talk to Nick today.

My phone vibrates in my back pocket and I slide it out. A text from my brother—not Nick.

Sorry I couldn't make it home this weekend, this experiment is killing me. Literally, it could kill me. Playing with virus is dangerous.

I crack a smile. Roberto can be a tad dramatic, but he's also a genius in physics and medicine and whatever else he touches. He's going to graduate from college two years early and save the world.

I type back: *Be careful.*

Always

I settle into my seat again, trying very hard to not remember what Roberto told me about the amount of viruses and bacteria and all that jazz crowding public transportation. A guy sitting two benches down is eating chicken tenders, and the scent surrounds me. I'm not hungry—not after eating lasagna with Nonna, but the smell reminds me of carefree evenings on the rooftop of Nick's house two years ago during Thanksgiving break. That's when our families still got along, and that's when we decided we didn't want to simply sit at their fancy table with their fancy meals and their fancy friends. We ordered KFC and climbed on the roof and talked all night. The three of us: Roberto, Nick and me.

A little girl with straight black hair and eyes slanting upwards enters the car with her mom. She has a big smile on her face and points to the seat in front of me. "Can we sit, Mommy?" Her mom nods.

They sit in front of me and the little girl snuggles up to her mom. Their purple jackets look similar with a snowman on the front pocket. The girl glances around and then she stands up to touch my bag.

"Lola," her mom calls and she sits back down, still staring at my bag.

Her face lights up and her grin turns wider. She reminds me of the kids on the poster for the Buddy Walk that was organized two weeks ago in the city to raise awareness about Down syndrome.

ALWAYS SECOND BEST

"Are you a ballerina?" she asks slowly with a laugh in her voice, her finger pointing to the pictures on my bag: ballet pointes and a dancer in a tutu.

"Yes, I am," I reply—trying to ignore the feeling in my gut that comes with the words. I don't know what it is, but it's unwelcome. I miss the joy that used to light my chest when I'd speak about dancing.

"I have Down syndrome," she says—very matter-of-fact, and before I can react she continues, "But I'm going to be a basketball player." Her mom kisses the top of her head.

"She's an amazing basketball player already." The mom winks. "But she also wants to be an ice skater and a lacrosse player and a gymnast, depending on what she sees on TV." She laughs. And a smile dances on my lips. They look so happy.

"I'm sure you'll be great," I tell her. She nods firmly as I wave goodbye. "This is my stop."

She waves back at me. "You're going to be great too!" And her vote of confidence means more to me than the latest "you can do it" speech I got from one of my teachers. Maybe because she seemed to believe it, while my teacher had a pity look on her face, the one that says, "I'm obligated to give you a pep talk, but in reality, you kind of suck."

The auditions are in three days. Three. Days.

I know I can do it. I know I have what it takes.

Note to self: work harder.

CHAPTER 2 - NICK

THE HOUSE SMELLS LIKE the apple pie our cook made for dinner last night: caramel and cinnamon. I think he took pity on me since our planned family dinner turned into a "Nick eats alone and plays video games all night" type of dinner. He knows apple pie with meringue is one of my favorite desserts. My true favorite dessert is the one Em made this summer: cannoli. Right before we started making out. She still had the taste of the Italian dessert on her lips.

I should remember not to think about Em, or about the way her kisses put fire in my veins, or about the way she felt in my arms. Because getting hard at my parents' house when they're only a few feet away is so not the way I want to end my weekend.

I shift on my feet and grab my bag, ready to head out without so much as a goodbye. I guess I'm still pissy after they ditched me yesterday. Most of my friends rave about the time they get to spend away from their parents, but that's much different when the time you get to spend with them is the exception to the rule. I wouldn't mind a few awkward dinners, a few questions about the school, my life. Something.

"You're already leaving?" Mom pops out of the living room, where she was on the phone for some fundraiser she's organizing in two months. She's not as sad as she used to be, but she's still not entirely present when she's home. The therapy sessions they drag me to at least once a month have helped, but it's like she focuses so much on mending her relationship with Daddy Dearest that she's not sure how to handle me. There are times when she reaches out to me, carves time in her busy schedule to talk to me and other times, when we barely see each other on weekends.

"It's late," I reply and rub the back of my neck. I'm much taller than her, but when she's looking at me a certain way, I revert back to my five-year-old self who didn't want to stray far from her. Back to when I believed my parents were heroes. I want to laugh at past-me and tell present-me to get a grip.

"I'm sorry we were so busy this weekend, but I promise next week, you and I will do something fun together."

"Okay." I don't hold my breath.

"How is Emilia doing these days?" she asks, narrowing her eyes at me like she's trying to read through my usual bullshit.

"She's doing well." I keep my tone as light as possible; even hearing Emilia's name feels like someone's punching me right in the chest. I fucked it all up and I don't know how to make it right. If I had a normal relationship with Mom, if Dad wasn't all set on me not dating Em, maybe I could ask her for advice. Em says she's seeing someone. I don't believe her…not because I think I'm irreplaceable but because she doesn't look happy. If she had moved on, she'd be happy. Right?

"I'm glad to hear that," she replies, touching a vase she received from the former governor of New York's wife, rearranging it slightly so it's perfectly in the middle of the small pedestal. I clench my fists. And it's my turn to really look at her: her lips are pursed as if she wants to say something else but doesn't while her hands are shaking a little, and they only shake when she's worried about something

"I…." My voice croaks like a thirteen-year-old boy's.

Her fingers trace the pattern of the vase—a blue flower. "We haven't seen her in a very long time," she says. I clench my fists harder, exhale loudly, trying to lift the pressure on my chest. Mom's doing better, and I don't want to push her away, to hamper her recovery, *our* recovery, by asking what's on the tip of my tongue. *Did you know?* My mind screams, begs her to read my thoughts. *Did you know Dad blackmailed me into dumping Emilia and dating other people—especially daughters of his buddies—to win a business deal?*

She tilts her head to the side. "We haven't seen Roberto in a long time either."

"They're busy. Everyone's busy." My tone is a bit more biting than intended. "Anyways, I have to go, but I'll be back next Friday night or Saturday." I force my lips into a short smile. The anger building up inside of me like a crescendo doesn't have much to do with Mom—it's more about me being a coward.

Every week, I tell myself I'm going to have the balls to confront Daddy Dearest. Every week, I brace myself to tell him I will no longer do as he tells me, that I won't give in to his blackmailing. No more dating girls because he says so. Every week, I fail. Either he's not home, or he's with Mom and she shouldn't become collateral damage. She seems so fragile at times, so ready to simply leave us behind and never look back.

Her phone rings and she raises a finger. "Wait a second," she tells me before picking up. Something about the fundraiser again. She puts her *nothing is wrong* mask on; her voice is stronger, but it's not happy. I'm pretty sure none of her so-called *luncheon friends* know about her problems.

My parents drag me to therapy "for the greater good of our family." I usually grunt a lot on the way there, but it's not all that bad. Mom apologized for leaving me behind when she needed time to think. She told me it wasn't about me, but it sure as hell felt that way when she packed up her bags and went on spacation for three months. I drove all the way to see her for her birthday, with Em holding my hand. Mine was early October and she didn't even call me. I told her that. She cried and my throat tightened so much I didn't think I was ever going to be able to breathe normally again.

"What do you want, Nicholas?" the therapist— Dr. Grahams—asked me during a grueling one-on-one session we all had to take before our family hour. I didn't answer, and he scribbled on his notepad. "Your desire to be accepted by your father should not overshadow your own needs, your own person," he said, and asked me to keep that in mind.

I'm trying to.

"Of course, Laura. You'll be the first to know," Mom says and rolls her eyes at the same time. "Listen, I have to go. Nick is about to leave for school."

I stare at her and then shift my bag to my other shoulder.

I don't want to ask Mom if she knows about Dad's blackmailing. Believing she didn't know is much easier. I need to believe one of my parents is not out there to use me.

She hangs up. "Tell Emilia hello from me," she says and I wince.

Way to sucker-punch me without knowing it, Mom.

"Sure thing," I reply. I've told Em I was sorry about how we ended things last summer. But I've never told her why. I've never told her how much I wish things were different. How much I want her back.

The therapist also told us of the importance of making amends, of how the truth would set us free.

Yeah, right.

Asking Mom if she knows about the blackmail gives me more jitters than the auditions coming up. But telling Em? Managing to do a butterfly—lifting myself off the floor as high as possible, twisting my body and landing gracefully on one knee—is nothing compared to spilling out the truth.

I can take the hate in her eyes, but not the hurt and the disgust.

ALWAYS SECOND BEST

Mom air-kisses me, landing a hand on my shoulder. She's definitely a bit more touchy-feely since we started therapy. "I know you've got a busy week coming with the auditions. And I know you wish your father would be more supportive."

"Understatement of the year." I drop my bag to the floor and cross my arms over my chest. *You're being defensive,* our therapist would say. I hesitate between mentally giving him the finger for intruding on my thoughts or shrugging because he's right.

"He's learning. He's doing better already."

True. Even with me, he's doing better. He hasn't asked me to date anyone for his business for the past three months. He's been much more careful around me, and he's been much more silent too, less pushy, less annoying, less everything. Definitely not more supportive, but not as destructive.

"You'll see. It's going to be a great year for you. For us. For our family." She touches my shoulder again. It's awkward but it's there.

"Okay, Mom. See you next week." And I do something I haven't done in such a long time. I bend down and press my lips to her cheek. "Love you, Mom."

Her hand flies to her face and her smile isn't fake. "Love you too, Son."

I can't remember the last time she's said it. I almost try to make a joke about it, anything to deflect the hope building inside of me, anything to not get hurt in the future if all goes down to shit again. But then I look at her and how she's trying, how she's opening up, how she's working hard on herself.

My lips turn up into a smile. Not the "I'm happy to leave this place" smile that I usually have when I go back to school.

This time it's a real, no-afterthought smile.

CHAPTER 3 - EM

LEAVING THE STUFFY subway behind, I climb the stairs to the Central Park exit. The cold air engulfs me. I tighten my scarf and put on my winter hat—Nick has the same one. They have our respective names on them. Nonna gave them to us for Christmas a few months ago, and talk about awkward around the tree when Nick opened his. He was there because his parents were in couples' therapy and Roberto begged Dad to let Nick spend Christmas with us. Dad wouldn't have agreed if Mom didn't plead his case.

I pretended to have a date on Christmas day with a mystery guy to avoid him. I pretended to have moved on. I pretended my heart didn't hurt seeing him sad.

I've done a lot of pretending since last summer.

I push the door of the School of Performing Arts. "Good evening," I tell the young receptionist who's working the weekend shift. She glances up from her magazine and waves—she's been there since February, apparently paying her way through grad school at NYU. The spotless entrance and the posters and brochures give way to narrow hallways. I turn to get into my dorm room. Some students go home on weekends, especially if, like me, their families live close by, but my roommate, Natalya, hasn't been home in a few months. She's supposed to fly back to Maine right after the auditions.

"Hey," I tell her as I enter our small room and carefully place my bag on the chair by my desk. The standard dorm room doesn't allow for much distraction: no TV, bunk beds, two desks and one big closet. And as usual, Nata's side is full of stuff while mine is spotless. Nata is glancing through pictures, her iPod buds in her ears. She takes them out and smiles.

"Hi. How was your weekend?" She puts up her long blonde hair in a messy ponytail that looks amazing on her.

"My weekend was good. I wanted to come back earlier to rehearse though, but didn't want to leave my Nonna."

"I get it. I wish I could have spent more time with my babushka." Nata's voice is sad and I want to kick myself in the butt for reminding her about her loss. Her grandmother passed away in January and it was a very tough time for her.

My mind fills with pictures of Nonna—laughing, hugging me, telling me she believes in me—and I hold on to those pictures, pushing away the way she looked on her hospital bed after her stroke last January: small, so small. And so fragile. I busy my hands with emptying my bag from the weekend and putting my dirty clothes in the hamper. I should have done my laundry at home, but spending time with Nonna was more important.

"Do you want to go grab something to eat at the cafeteria?" Nata asks. I sometimes bring her food from Nonna's restaurant, but she's super careful with what she eats. I should be too.

"No, thanks. I've got a few things to do," I reply, pointing to my laptop. "Got to make sure I ace some of the classes, in case I don't get a part in the showcase."

"You're going to get one, and an amazing one," Nata says. She doesn't say the best one because, well, when you're competing for the number one spot, you only wish it for yourself. "Do you want me to bring you anything?"

"I'm fine. I ate lasagna before coming back, but thanks."

"Sure. I won't be long." She glances behind her shoulder. "I'll pick up the mess when I get back, promise."

My lips turn up into my *I don't believe you but it's okay* smile and I reply, "Yeah, yeah. Whatever."

"I promise I will. I had to rehearse a lot this weekend. I couldn't get myself high enough in the air for a simple *grand jeté*." She sighs. "No matter how many times I tried, my body wouldn't cooperate."

"I'm sure you managed at the end."

"It was okay, but not perfect." She smiles slightly and closes the door behind her. Nata's not only gorgeous, she's also well on her way to becoming the first junior ever to get the main role in a showcase.

I pick up one of her books and put it on her nightstand, sliding the picture of her and her best friend a bit to the side. They're jumping into a lake, laughing and holding hands.

At school she's so much more reserved. Some students think she's shy, others believe she's full of herself because she's gorgeous and talented—with her blonde hair falling down past her shoulders, her blue eyes, the way she lights up the scene as soon as she steps into it—but most either want to be her or be with her. Nata and I have been roommates for three years, and she's one of my only friends here—but even I don't really know what's been going on and why she's been looking down.

I sit back at my desk. Maybe I should have gone with Nata to the canteen to keep her company, but another reason we've been pretty good roommates is that we give each other some space.

I inhale deeply, count to three and click on a document entitled "Letter – Fourth draft." I've been working on it for three weeks, and it's still not ready. I need to get every word right, and that has nothing to do with any school assignments.

It's a letter for my birth mother.

Dear Claire,

I hope it's okay I call you Claire. My name's Emilia, that's the name my parents gave me. I'm not sure why I'm writing this letter.

I'm not sure if you'll even read it, but I want to tell you a story. A story about me and maybe, you'll decide that you do want to meet me after all.

I simply want to understand.

I erase "I simply want to understand." I delete the first lines. I don't need to tell her my name. She knows me, she knows my name. She knows my entire family. She used to be my father's secretary, after all.

I reread all the words out loud. Slowly. My voice sounds way too mechanic, too detached, and the words don't compute. They're not enough. They don't explain the void I've felt inside ever since she slammed her door in my face.

When I thought about finding my birth mother, our imaginary reunion was full of smiling and hugging and talking and laughing.

Instead, my heart exploded in a thousand pieces that I don't think I'll ever manage to tape back together. I don't think she could have run away from me faster than she did when I tried to talk to her last summer, and if she'd slammed the door of her car any harder, it would have been destroyed.

Like my feelings.

I tap my fingers on the desk, get up, sit back down, stare at the screen.

The memories of last summer scream in my ears. How Dad got tired of my digging around, of me asking questions. How my heart dropped at my feet and took forever to find its place in my chest again when he finally told me the truth. That my birth mother wanted to sell me to the highest bidder, how he bought me from her, how he'd been lying to me all those years.

I minimize the window and go into the folder I named "Truth folder."

Over the summer, we—Nick and me—found next to nothing about Claire, but it's amazing what a bit of money can do. So many sites gather information on people. And it doesn't hurt that I found her social security number in Dad's old office paperwork.

I reread the file. Her parents died in a car accident when she was young. She pulled herself and her little sister through college. She worked several jobs then, but after college seemed to be doing pretty well for herself.

The loud buzz of my alarm startles me, reminding me I need to do some stretching exercises. I close the document, then the folder. My finger hovers for two seconds before closing the letter without even saving it. Sending this letter would be stupid, ridiculous, desperate. I need one that might convince her talking to me is a must.

My alarm rings again and I reach out for my phone. It's almost eight p.m.—Nata's going to be back soon. Nick should be in his room now. Unless he's out with another girl. Yet again.

The churning in my stomach hasn't receded; it's still as strong as the first time I saw him after breaking things off last summer.

I was running late. For the first time ever. I turned in the hallways to make it to our first school assembly meeting of the year and there he was leaning against the wall, Jen snuggling against him. I muffled a scream and fought back tears.

Two weeks before, his lips were on mine, his arms were around my waist, his fingers were trailing up and down my back.

ALWAYS SECOND BEST

They weren't kissing, but it was clear they were back together. I had heard the rumors, I had seen tweets, but I didn't want to believe it. We had agreed we would only have one summer together: one summer that was supposed to be easy. After all, the terms were simple: he didn't want to have a relationship once school started because he wanted to concentrate on his career, plus with our parents not getting along and my brother breathing down our neck, it made sense to keep it limited.

I was not supposed to fall even more in love with him, I was not supposed to get my heart broken. I was not supposed to hope we would forget about the expiration date on our relationship and keep going.

But when everything went crashing faster than a dancer missing his or her landing, I still had hope. I dreamed that he'd come and knock at my door, that he'd tell me he was sorry, that he'd fight for me.

Note to self: stop being delusional.

"Hi!" Jen had called my name and waved with the biggest and most triumphant smile on her face.

Nick opened his mouth but he didn't say a word.

We stared at each other. I thought I saw regret in his eyes, but most likely he was only squinting to figure out if I was mad or not. I swallowed my pain and my pride, and I waved at them. Like it didn't slice my heart in two to see them together.

Whatever. It's been eight months. I'm over it. And even if I wasn't over it, I wouldn't let myself get hurt like this again.

The only way for me to come out of all this on top is to get the starring role at this year's showcase. I have the scenario in my head. I get the main part and I send another letter to my birth mother; she's so proud she comes to see me. I get the main part and Nick finally realizes we're right for one another. I get the main part and my parents look at me with as much pride as when Roberto told them he won a scholarship to spend a summer at MIT next year.

I stare at the dark computer screen.

I see my future. I see what I want, what I need.

I get up. My muscles tense and flex with determination.

This main part is mine.

CHAPTER 4 - NICK

THE WIND SLAPS ME in the face and I shiver. It's supposed to be spring in a few days, but we've been stuck in this shitty winter weather for weeks. I grab the hat in my coat pocket—it's the one Nonna gave me at Christmas. I know she was trying to patch things up between Em and me. But maybe Em thought Nonna knew it was going to be a cold winter and we both needed a hat. Matching hats.

I could have asked the chauffeur to drive me back to school. Last year, I never asked, because it was one way to spend time with Em. Back when it was easy between us, before our summer, before I admitted to myself that she's more to me than just a friend.

Now, I don't ask because it's one more statement that I don't need my father's money.

I walk in front of Em's former house—the doorman is still the same, and he waves at me before blowing on his hands. I wave back, wishing I had thought about grabbing some gloves. Snow flurries fall steadily.

Em used to love the snow. She used to love making snowmen in Central Park.

Every year, we'd ice skate with all the tourists. She'd hold my hand and I'd pretend it didn't mean anything more than friends having fun.

I'm tired of pretending.

I kick a rock from the sidewalk.

I haven't told Dr. Grahams about the blackmailing, but Em did come up during one of our sessions. Dad must have bitten his tongue pretty hard, because he didn't say how he believes Em and her family aren't good enough.

I push the door to The School of Performing Arts. My feet take me to Em's room. I want to knock. I want to talk to her. I need to talk to her, about my parents, about school, about the latest TV show I'm recording for when we have time to watch TV again. And then I want to tell her again I'm sorry, tell her I hope I'm not too late, beg her to take me back.

I'm tempted to call Rob and ask him for advice, but he'd tell me to figure this shit out by myself, that he's Em's brother and will stay out of our business—unless I hurt her again, in which case he would punch me in the face. And I'm convinced he would. And I'd probably let him. I don't ever want to hurt Em again.

I'll never forget the look on Em's face the first day back at school after our summer together. How sad she looked, how lost and how angry.

It took everything in me to not go and pull her to me, to not apologize, to not kiss her tears away.

ALWAYS SECOND BEST

Instead of knocking, I shake my head and stride to my dorm room. I drop my stuff on my bed. My roommate must be rehearsing or at the cafeteria because he's nowhere to be seen. His clothes are there and his mega-poster of his boyfriend—a former student at the school—is back on the wall. After they had a fight last week, he took the poster down, claiming it was over.

Looks like they made up.

I stroll to the cafeteria and spot Em's roommate. She's hard to miss with that shiny blonde hair, and she's just the type of person you notice right away.

"Hey, Nata," I tell her. She's hesitating between the fish of the day and salad. But then ends up getting a yogurt and an apple.

"Hi," she replies. "How was your weekend?" She grabs a spoon and a water bottle.

"Nothing special. Played video games, tried to cram for a history exam we have on Tuesday. You'd think we would be given some sort of class amnesty during the week of the auditions."

"Our class actually has important until April."

"Nice." She sits at a table and I pull out the chair opposite of her. "How is Em doing?" I ask and rub the back of my neck. I sound like the biggest pussy in the world.

"She seems to be doing okay. Stressed but okay." She takes a sip of her water. "You could ask her, you know. I thought you guys were talking more often again."

"We are." And it's true, we found some sort of truce, but it's a painful one: the more time I spend around her, the more I miss her, and the more I can't seem to tell her.

"Hmm." Nata bites into her apple. She doesn't say another word. I don't know if Em told her about our friends-with-limited-benefits pact from this summer. And I won't ask. If Em wants to talk to her, she can and she should, but I'm not going to start rumors or spread anything Em doesn't want me to.

Nata looks lost in her own little world. Her long blonde hair falls freely on her shoulders and she's tapping her foot, probably without even realizing it. She's surely rehearsing her choreography in her mind.

I clear my throat. "Has Em said..?" I stop myself. Asking Nata about Em sounds wrong. "Never mind."

Nata nods as if she could actually hear my internal dialogue and agreed with it. She watches me. "Em misses you. I know she does," she whispers and I'm not sure I heard her correctly, but then her lips stretch into a small, encouraging smile. "I don't know what happened between you two, but I'm pretty sure it's fixable."

I'm about to protest, when she stands up. "I know it's not my business, but it's only fixable if you actually talk. And not tiptoe around each other like you're dancing *Swan Lake*." She pauses. "But don't screw it up for her right before the audition. It's important to her. It's important to all of us."

"I know."

"Good." She nods one more time and with her head high, she walks out of the cafeteria.

I inhale deeply. My entire body hums with anticipation. I can do this.

ALWAYS SECOND BEST

I can face Em, face my parents, face my demons.

CHAPTER 5 - EM

ORGANIZING MY SIDE of the room—and
sometimes Natalya's—always calms me down. But
tonight, I wish my hands were deep in cookie dough,
or cannoli dough or something else to help me.
Because my entire body feels too full of nervous
energy to go to sleep. Even after rehearsing for an
hour, the usual exhaustion is mixed with anticipation.

For the audition? For Nick? I look forward to
seeing him. Old habits die hard, as Roberto would say,
when he lit up one cigarette after Giovanni left in
October. I called him on his bullshit though, because
he hadn't had a cigarette in more than three years.
He'd smoked for six months when he was fifteen, until
Dad caught him and forced him to go volunteer at a
cancer center. That's also where Roberto developed
his love for science.

Nata enters the room and plops herself on her
bed. "I saw Nick at the canteen," she says, watching
me way too carefully. Nata breathes ballet; she usually

doesn't fall into the school's gossip mill, and she hasn't asked me anything about Nick. Ever. "He wanted to ask about you," she says.

"He wanted to or he did?" I raise an eyebrow.

"I suck at trying to help people and, you know, pretty much at socializing with other people when it's not about dancing. I know I do. All I'm going to say is that you miss him and he misses you and I know you're saying you need to concentrate on the auditions, but if you're miserable dancing *Sleeping Beauty*, the judges will see it."

I sink into my chair. Nata and I usually only talk about classes and ballet, and maybe the occasional quick discussion about our families. She's been struggling with her parents this semester, and with the death of her grandmother and working so hard, she barely has the time to breathe.

I grab my laptop, sit down next to her and nudge her shoulder with mine. "Thanks," I tell her. "Do you want to watch the interview of Misty Copeland that aired on CBS? I'm pretty sure it's uploaded to their website already."

"We probably should go to sleep," Nata says. She stretches her arm above her head and smiles. "But watching an accomplished ballerina is almost like rehearsing." She scoots back on the bed and leans against the wall. "Thirty minutes, max." But she smiles, and we end up watching the entire interview.

The second dance class of the day isn't my favorite one, and it's even more difficult to focus since I slept like crap. Since Nata mentioned she saw Nick and how she thought he wanted to ask about me, I expected him to text me or call me or even pass by our room.

But he didn't.

And I've been going back and forth about sending yet another letter to my birth mom. I've sent one already and it didn't get me anywhere. The last one sucked big time and she probably ripped it up into tiny pieces. It also got me a stern lecture from my father about respecting people's boundaries and not hurting my mother's feelings. I stretch my arms above my head, forcing myself to be in the moment and not in the swirling thoughts of my mind.

There's a buzz in the room. The energy of everyone is multiplied a thousand times: the fear, the excitement, the desire to succeed. You can see all of that in the tight smiles, in the few encouraging words, in the way people position themselves before the rehearsal.

What used to be routine and mandatory is now another way to shine, to show the teachers and the School that we're "it."

Everybody's concentrated on their movements. Everybody's prepping for the auditions in three days. Everybody seems so sure of themselves.

And then, there's me. Standing awkwardly, not sure where to put my hands. Already above my head? On my waist? Which position would scream "ballerina" to the world and to my professor?

I'm in line, waiting for my turn to perform the choreography in front of the class and our professor, trying very hard to concentrate and visualize each movement. But my eyes keep on dancing toward the corner of the room, where Nick stands, waiting for his turn, talking with Kayode and Carla, laughing like everything is well in the world. Maybe in his world, everything's fine. In mine: not so much.

I miss him so much it's physically painful. And why does he have to look so good? His arm muscles are more defined than ever and I'm pretty sure he grew taller. I remember how it felt to be wrapped in his embrace, how my body was on the verge of combusting, and my heart on the verge of falling right into his chest, to find a spot next to his heart to cuddle.

I shake my head, force my eyes to focus on Nata, who's in the middle of the room, dancing the short routine our instructor Svetlana asked her to show us.

Note to lips: stop wanting to kiss Nick.
Note to self: stop being delusional.

I relax my shoulders, take a deep breath.

I watch how Nata angles her arms over her head, how she reaches that moment of perfection and bliss in the air as she jumps into a *grand jeté*.

How she makes it look so easy and yet so beautiful and full of emotion.

I purse my lips; my stomach is in tight knots and my entire body buzzes. Nick's watching me. He's watching me and nods one time, our code to tell me I can do it. But I don't answer. I turn away. I do not will myself to appear even calmer than usual and I do not cross my fingers, hoping Nick notices I'm wearing the leather bracelet he gave me for my birthday two years ago. Because if I did hope, that would mean I still care too much about him, that I didn't learn anything last summer, that I'm still hoping for us to find a way to be together.

"Emilia," our instructor Svetlana calls me. "Can you come here for a second?" Her usual smile is replaced with a way-too-serious frown.

I glance around—everyone is looking at me. My stomach clenches, but I force my lips into a small smile. Pretending I'm not worried at all. Always pretending. I pass in front of Jen, who pretends whispers, "Oooh, hope everything is okay" in a tone that says she hopes I'm going to break my leg.

Bitch.

There're no other words. She dated Nick right after our summer together and got pissed when he dumped her three weeks later. Didn't she get the memo? Didn't she remember that's exactly what happened to her freshman year? Nick dated her for an entire two weeks before moving on. Since then she's hated me. Like it was my fault.

Nick used to change girlfriends faster than he'd spin a pirouette.

Jen scowls at me before turning all her attention to Nick, who's not even acknowledging her. Silly, silly her. Some girls never learn. The pang in my chest deepens, cuts through, right into my heart—I'm not *some girls*… I've learned, and the lesson has been painful.

"Emilia, you seem distracted. Is everything okay?" Svetlana's hand touches my shoulder gently. She sounds worried. She's one of those teachers that you want to please, that you want to try your hardest for, that you want to make proud.

ALWAYS SECOND BEST

"I'm fine. It's the excitement, that's all," I reply, noticing even from here that Nick's striding our way. "I should get back in line," I blabber.

"Are you sure? Have you eaten enough?" Svetlana continues and the palm of her hand touches my forehead. "Are you feeling okay? You look flushed."

"I'm fine. Really, don't worry." And I smile. It's probably the worst smile in history, but I don't stop to check if Svetlana buys it. I turn on my heels and get back in line. I brush past Nick and everything turns slow motion except my heart beats faster and my palms get clammy and this is ridiculous. Nick and I used to be great friends, best friends. We used to talk and argue and laugh. We used to kiss for hours. I'm tempted to look back to see if his eyes are on me or not, but I take a deep breath and keep walking.

And soon enough it's my turn.

And I will myself to be the best, to impress Svetlana, to impress everyone. I need to get the main role in this year's showcase. The competition is tough but I've been working my ass off. That's all I've been doing.

And I perform as I'm supposed to. I raise my arms, stretch my legs, jump, land on one foot, propel myself in a pirouette, and. I dance.

But not with my heart.

And it shows.

CHAPTER 6 - NICK

HER SMILE IS ALL fucking wrong; her posture and the way she arches herself may be almost perfect, but she's stripped of all emotions. She's supposed to show how sad she is in those movements, but I know her. She won't let a drop of sadness escape because she's scared as shit it will only be the beginning, that she'll break down during her performance, that she won't be able to pretend any longer. Natalya is watching her too and she purses her lips. She sees the same thing I do: technique but no passion. In our career, if we don't have the passion, we won't get as far, but we'll kill ourselves trying, always trying and never succeeding.

"Are you okay?" I ask Em as she finishes and she nods, muttering an "I'm fine" that wouldn't convince anyone. Especially not me. I know her better than I know myself, and I know her smiles and her tones and the way her lips taste.

ALWAYS SECOND BEST

I can't push her. Not right now. Not in class. Not here.

We found a thin balance, a balance that's threatening to tilt one way or the other every second, but a balance nonetheless. If she's really moved on, I'll respect that. I'll beat my head against a fucking wall for losing her in the first place, but if she's happy, then fine. But she doesn't look happy and I've never seen the guy she said she was seeing at Christmas. And it wouldn't be the first time she's pretended she's fine.

"Nicholas!" Svetlana calls my name and it seems it's not the first time, because she claps her hands like she does when she's trying to get our attention.

I get into my zone and concentrate on making sure my jumps are the highest possible, that all my muscles are focused on the choreography. I need Em, but I also need to land this audition. This audition could mean a lead in the showcase. A lead in the showcase would not only be the best way to shut Daddy Dearest up, but it would also mean I might get discovered, get a spot in a famous ballet company, live the future of my dreams.

"Good job, Nick," Svetlana says when I've finished my routine. Jen slides next to me, her hand on my forearm like we're used to touching one another. Maybe we used to be. Maybe a lifetime ago, but I've never made her promises I couldn't keep. I've never told her that we'd stay together forever.

"Do you have time to help me out tonight?" Jen uses her flirtatious voice—it's so low I have trouble hearing her. Before, I would have leaned forward, but that's what she wants. And I've been trying to establish some boundaries. My dear father uses me like a pawn in his business deals, including charming the girls of some of his biggest clients. If they're happy and gush to their parentals, my father feels like he has a better chance of winning. Jen's one of those girls. Nothing more.

"Nick?" Jen asks again.

"I don't know yet," I answer and I kind of hate myself for being curt with her. She doesn't deserve it. It's not her fault she's not Emilia.

And the way Jen flinches, the way she steps back, trying to keep her smile on, the way she glances away, I know she's hurting. She's been hurting.

I sigh. "Fine. Let's see if one of the rooms is available tonight," I say and her eyes are too bright, too hopeful so I add, "Thirty minutes, max."

She nods and when I turn around, I catch Em watching me—she looks disappointed.

No matter what I do, I can't win.

CHAPTER 7 - EM

THE END OF CLASSES can't come fast enough.
Seeing Jen lean toward Nick, seeing her touch his arm,
seeing how she smiled at me and let me know they
have a date tonight shouldn't hurt as much as it does.
I'm the one who suggested he and I tried a limited
Friends-with-Certain-Benefits arrangement for a few
weeks. I'm the one who told him we should cool it off.
I'm the one who said we needed distance when school
started again because we both needed to concentrate
on what's important: dancing.

And I'm the one who keeps on pretending that
I'm absolutely fine with everything—even inventing a
fake boyfriend.

I slide on the treacherous sidewalk, holding
myself on the lamp pole. Snow flurries fall steadily
and most of the people have determined looks on their
faces, a certain angle their bodies as if nothing could
stop them from hurrying to their destinations. Some

mutter about the weather being totally crazy for March, that winter needs to stop. A few are enjoying the snow. One couple is holding a little girl by the hand and they're laughing. Picture of the happy family. My chest squeezes, but it's not as painful to think about my own birth mother now as it was last summer, right after she slammed her car door on me.

I raise my face to the sky, letting the snow wet my lips, wet my cheeks, taking a deep breath. Darkness settles on the city and like every night, I walk all the way to Central Park. I thought the place where Nick and I kissed for the last time eight months ago would be painful, but it's not. It's a place where I can sit and call Nonna, where I can let my tears fall, where I can let myself be me.

The snow covers the grass and the fountain isn't working. I tighten my heavy snow coat around me and lean against a tree. I grab my cell from my pocket and dial Nonna's number.

"Hi, Bellisima, how are you? Thanks again for passing by yesterday," Nonna answers and I hate how frail her voice is.

"I'm coming over this weekend again. Promise. I wish I could pass by during the week, but we have the audition in three days and you know how it is."

"You're going to do amazing, I know it. I wish you could come earlier, but I understand." She sounds happy but out of breath. Her stroke five months ago changed her. Even though she hates to admit it. She coughs. "Roberto's been pining over that Italian boy who went back to his country and he's been studying way too hard. He only has time to come give me a kiss every night, but he doesn't stick around for long."

ALWAYS SECOND BEST

"I know, Nonna. But Mom's with you." I take a deep breath. Every single time I think about something worse happening to her, tears spring to my eyes and my heart squeezes so tightly I can't breathe.

"Your mom is an angel, Bellisima. She's an angel," Nonna says and my lips turn up—even with everything that's happened with my parents, they both have been trying so hard to be supportive. Especially Mom.

"How is Mr. Edwards?" I change the topic to something Nonna usually smiles about: their relationship started about the same time Nick's and mine did…whatever we did last summer. But unlike us, they didn't have a "best used by" stamp on their relationship.

"Ben is doing great. He brought me flowers today and he promised to bring me tomatoes from his garden this summer. He told me his garden is the best in all of New York City," she tells me. "And I believe him."

"Did he ask you to marry him again?"

Nonna chuckles. "He did. And I said no. But he'll ask again next week. I'm not sure if he really wants me to say yes—it might stop the fun if I do."

"I love you, Nonna," I tell her and my hand grips the phone tighter. "I'll see you this weekend, okay?" I don't want to hang up but I have to. I have to go back to the School and I have to get some sleep. If I don't sleep enough, I'll be sluggish. If I'm sluggish, I won't perform as well as I should—like earlier today. And if I perform as badly as today, I can get used to the title of "Always Second Best."

I hurry back to my room and settle at the desk. Nata's not back yet—she's probably rehearsing or talking to her parents, maybe.

I grab a piece of paper with the School Of Performing Arts logo on it and start writing. Not thinking, only feeling.

Dear Claire,

I'm sorry to have surprised you last August. I was afraid you didn't want to see me and I didn't even bother to ask you, to warn you. Nothing.

I've already written a letter to you, but I'm not sure you received it and it wasn't a great letter. I'm not saying this one is better. But I'm trying.

I'm happy. Most of the time. I'm a dancer. A ballerina. I've wanted to become a ballerina ever since I was old enough to understand that my birth mother had wrapped me into a pink blanket with a ballerina on it. I thought you might want to know that. My adoptive parents are wonderful – I mean, you know them. I love them.

I'd like to understand what happened. I'd like to understand why you didn't want me, why you tried to sell me to the highest bidder. I'd like to maybe know a bit more about your family. All I could find was that your parents passed away in an accident and you have a little sister and kids of your own. The reason I want to know so badly is that sometimes I can't help but wonder if there's something of you in me. I can't help but wonder who I am.

I am not saying you have all the answers. I am not saying you should even tell me anything.

ALWAYS SECOND BEST

I just want you to know that I'd like to meet you again or talk to you.

On your terms. On the phone, per letters, whatever.

Please.
Emilia

I don't reread it.

I know Nata keeps envelopes and stamps close by—she used to write to her grandmother almost every week before she passed away. I dig through her mess, feeling slightly guilty about it. And find them by her pile of dirty laundry. Because clearly, that's their place.

I put the stamp on the envelope, write down Claire Carter's address, but instead of going directly to the mailbox, I find myself taking the hallway that leads to Nick's dorm. He'd understand why I'm writing another letter, and I've been fighting the urge to call him for weeks now. He must know my story about having a boyfriend was bullshit. I know he's not much on social media, but there's not one mention of me going out with anyone anywhere. And if he asked Roberto, I'm pretty sure Roberto told him I've been a recluse since August.

Nick's been trying, really trying to talk to me and he apologized. Twice. But he never said the words I need to hear.

I'm imagining the scene. I'm going to knock on his door and he's going to pull me to him and kiss me before I can finish my sentence, then we'll laugh and he'll take my hand into his and he'll tell me how sorry he is for how things ended between us, and then we'll talk. All night.

My lips stretch into a smile and the flutters in my belly are dancing to their own hopeful rhythm

I turn the corner to his dorm room, hold my breath.

And my heart deflates like a sad popped balloon.

He's going in his room.

With Jen.

CHAPTER 8 - NICK

DANCING WITH JEN is pointless—she's ready. Sweat pearls down my forehead as I lift her up in the air. She's extending her right leg and her arms, and she manages to make it look like it's the easiest move ever. And it's super difficult. Her entire body needs to be committed, her mind needs to be on the movement.

I slowly turn and then gather her in my arms; her back is arched and once more she's perfect.

As soon as her feet hit the floor, she throws her arms around me. "Thanks! If you get the part and I get the part, we're going to be amazing." She inches even closer so her entire body is aligned against mine. Her hand slowly goes down my back—and I invented that move.

I clear my throat. "You're going to do great." I turn around to pick up my sweater and put it on. "We should go back to the dorms. I need to do a few things and it's late already."

"We could hang out," she says. "We haven't hung out in forever." She steps closer to me again.

I purse my lips, narrow my eyes and shake my head, trying to keep my voice as nice as possible. I don't want to hurt her feelings, I really don't. "I'm busy. And I think we both know we're not going to hang out like we used to."

Her mouth opens and then closes and then she straightens herself. Back to the I-never-get-hurt Jen attitude. "Let's go." She pouts and leads the way, keeping some distance between us, until we reach the dorms.

I'm about to say bye to her, when she stops in her tracks. "Do you mind if I borrow one of your videos?" she asks.

"What video?" I check the time on my cell again—we've been gone for almost an hour.

"The one from last year's auditions."

"Don't you have it too? Didn't they upload on the server?"

"I have shitty reception--the Wi-Fi signal sucks in my room." She tilts her head to the side and bats her eyelashes in a very non-Jen way. "Please, that'd be super helpful. I need to look at how I can improve." Her voice is pleading and she still sounds a bit unsure of herself. Despite rarely showing any weakness.

I sigh. "Fine, come on in for a sec." I open the door. She follows me inside my dorm and waves at my roommate Kayode.

Kayode points to the computer where he's skyping with his boyfriend in California. "Mark says hi." Mark's voice is a bit muffled, but he sounds happy. He's one year older than Kayode and graduated last year. Kayode's hoping to get into a ballet company close by. Otherwise, he said he'd try to dance in music videos, maybe attempt acting in Hollywood. He's got it all figured out.

Lucky him.

Jen stares at my desk and her mouth turns into a silent "o." I glance at what she's staring at: the collage Em made me for my birthday two years ago. And then there's a selfie I took of the both of us during the summer. Em is leaning on me, kissing my cheek and my smile is wide, I-can't-believe-I'm-this-lucky wide. I don't think I've ever smiled like this with anyone else.

"Here's the video." I give her the USB stick that has all the videos of the past three years of showcases. I always make sure to download them whenever they're put on the server. I'm surprised Jen hasn't done the same. Or maybe she has and it's yet another plot to spend more time together.

"Thanks," she replies, still staring at the picture.

Kayode laughs in the background at something Mark must have told him.

"I have to go," Jen continues and I open the door for her, but before I can close it, she throws her arms around my neck. "Thanks again." Her hug lingers and I'm the one to break it off.

"Jen, come on," I mutter and she steps back, but still so close that we're almost touching. Her hand is on my shoulder and she tilts her head as if she's expecting me to kiss her. Not going to happen.

"It's just…" She opens her mouth, closes it again. "Never mind." She holds the USB up. "Thanks again for that. And I'll see you tomorrow." She clears her throat. "Em's an idiot. Clearly, I am too. But she's a bigger one. I wouldn't let you go."

I shake my head and watch her disappear into the hallway.

She doesn't know. Em's not the one who fucked everything up.

I did.

I plop myself on my bed.

"You look like shit, man," Kayode tells me. He types while he speaks, having switched from Skype to G-chatting with Mark. "What happened?"

"Nothing, just Jen."

Kayode laughs. "Yes, poor Nick. All those girls throwing themselves at you. Must be tough. And some of the guys too. I remember Mark having a huge crush on you before realizing I was the one for him." He checks me out. "I get it, you're hot." He smiles. "Dark hair, green eyes, a body to die for and that smile of yours is pretty sexy too."

"Hmm, thanks?" I raise an eyebrow.

"And I know every girl thought they could be the one to change you, to make you fall in love with them and forget everyone else. I think it's the show business—we have to believe in fairy tales."

"I wasn't that bad."

"Yes, you were. But with that monk thing you have going on since this January? I think they're even hotter for you. You've never been a jerk, but now it's even more forbidden fruit, or that someone-could-make-me-smile again face and maybe it's you."

"Whatever. Before you started going out with Mark, you swore you wouldn't get tied down."

"I was searching for love," he says. "Plus, being the only black guy in this school, I was a prize to be had."

"Whatever." My cell buzzes. "You broke more hearts than I did."

Kayode shrugs. "Maybe, but it's not because I was avoiding the one I really wanted. Once Mark and I got together, I stopped being stupid. Can't say the same for you." He smiles as if to take the sting off his words and then turns back to his computer.

My cell buzzes again and this time I check my messages.

Roberto's texting me: How is Em doing?

He knows Em and I have been weird with one another since this summer. We're still talking, and we're still polite but we no longer have hours-long conversations, we try not to be alone together. We haven't played a single video game since October, and that was because Rob made us play with him.

I type back.

Nick: She seemed a bit out of it.

Rob: She's worried about Nonna. Can you keep an eye on her?

I raise an eyebrow to the ceiling.

Nick: I thought you wanted me to lose a limb and have vultures eat my eyes for making Em cry last summer, and apparently during Winter Break.

Rob: Don't remind me.

My phone rings—it's more like Rob to call than to type. "I thought you hated texting," I answer.

Rob sighs. "I used to. But texting and sexting is pretty much all Giovanni and I have nowadays. Not much more."

"How is he doing?" I ask. Giovanni is Roberto's longest relationship, and they've only seen each other three times since last August. Giovanni came over in October for a conference, then in December for Christmas, and Roberto traveled to Italy a few weeks ago. For only five days. And he saved the entire year for that trip.

"He's doing well. Now, if I could convince him to come out to his parents, maybe it'd be even better."

"I'm sorry."

"I thought Europeans were supposed to be more progressive on this type of stuff. I mean even Ireland got the marriage-for-all before we did. But apparently, the Catholic Church is still split on the concept of love. Whatever... I'm a non-believer, but it's important for Giovanni." He takes a deep breath. "Thanks for asking by the way, but it's really about Em. Ever since Nonna's stroke, she's worried, even though the doctors say Nonna had a great recovery and she's doing much better."

"I'm glad she's better."

"Thanks. On top of that, Em's been kind of down lately.

"She wrote at least one letter to that woman, and I'm pretty sure she's going to write at least once more." Rob doesn't like to call Em's birth mother by her real name—he's still mad at the way she treated Em when she went to meet her.

My brain processes his words. "Wait. She did?" It hurts to think she didn't even let me know. I was there when she went to visit her for the first time.

"She did. And she told my parents and my dad got super angry. Super mad."

"When was that?"

"Two weeks ago."

"Your dad visited my dad two weeks ago."

"They're talking again?"

I nod. I was surprised too. Ever since my father fired Em and Rob's dad, they haven't been the best of friends. "It would seem like it. Listen, I'll try to talk to Em."

"Just take care of her. Let her know you're there for her. I know she misses you." Rob clears his throat. "And it hurts me to say this, but you were good for her. Now, if only you didn't stomp on her heart like you did."

"I told you I was sorry," I reply. And I am. Em and I had agreed to only be together for one summer, but I wanted so much more. However, when Daddy Dearest asked me to go out with Jen, I couldn't say no. He blackmailed me into it. He threatened to step down as a member of the School of Performing Arts Foundation, but most importantly, he promised to give me information about Em's birth mother if I stopped seeing Em, if I simply let it go. He was involved in the entire adoption, drawing the legal paperwork—he was part of the secret. He knew everything.

I rub the back of my neck. "If I could change what happened, you know that I would." Last summer, I convinced myself this was the only solution, that I wasn't good enough for Em anyway. That we couldn't be together. That we would be making a mistake. Leaving her was the big fucking mistake. Not telling her the truth was the big fucking mistake. Not standing up to my father was the big fucking mistake.

Rob coughs and takes a deep breath. "I know you're sorry. If you weren't, I wouldn't get you involved in all of this. Just don't screw it up again."

"I'm really trying not to."

"Anyways, are you ready for tomorrow?"

"I think so," I answer.

"You're going to nail your audition. You'll see."

"If I do, we need to go out and celebrate or you need to come to my place and play the new Soccer World game that came out last week."

"Sounds like a plan," he replies.

I clear my throat. "So, that guy Em mentioned at Christmas…that Andrew. Are they still together? Is it serious?"

"Not my business, dude. If you want to talk to Em, you talk to her about it, but I'm not going to be your spy or your informant. Forget it." He yawns. "I should go to bed soon. I've been feeling crappy for the past week or so. Some virus that doesn't want to let go. Thanks again for checking up on her. It means a lot." Before I can reply, he hangs up.

Kayode sits on his bed and clears his throat loudly. "I need to say something else, and it's not that I wish Rob instead of Em decided to become a dancer and share his room with me. Yes, Roberto is hot. But that's not the point." Kayode mumbles and then yawns loudly. "You might not want to hear it."

"What?"

"You need to grow a pair and talk to the girl. Em's not going to bite. And if she bites, you might like it."

"Since when are you a guru of relationships?"

"Since I am dating the rising star of the California Ballet. I just got an email from him. Mark got his solo!" He claps his hands and I smile.

"Impressive! Congrats!" I give him a quick hug. Mark and Kayode are good for each other.

"Thanks but don't change the topic."

"I've tried to talk to her."

"No. You tried to make out with the only friend she has here during the New Year's Eve party."

"I didn't... Not really."

"You didn't. But that's not what Em thinks. The rumor that got to her ears was that you and Nata fucked like rabbits in the coat closet. Never mind that Natalya has virgin written on her forehead. You're lucky I have a big heart and hate seeing you both so depressed. I did tell her you didn't do anything...but still."

"Jen asked me if we had sex and I said no. I haven't had sex in months. I didn't even kiss her. I didn't do anything. It was right after Em told me she was dating someone new and seriously while I thought we were making progress. I really thought we'd get back together during Christmas."

"It's cute how you still believe in Santa Claus. Em doesn't know that and on top of it, I don't think that's an accomplishment she's going to fall at your feet for. You were with Jen right after her, and then you dated Tasha and Sandra."

"Tasha was only for a week. And I didn't really date Sandra, I took her to one gala."

"The gala Em had been talking about for weeks."

As if I didn't already feel bad enough.

"Talk to her," Kayode says. "You'll regret it if you don't."

I'm scared shitless that if I do talk to her, if I tell her everything, she's going to push me away, and it's so much easier to believe that she won't than to face the reality she might. But Kayode is right. I nod, take my phone and text her. "I'll text you in the morning to make sure you're up," I type. I used to do that a lot last year. She's not the easiest to move and get ready in the morning, and I'd text her with a funny picture to make sure she was up. "Maybe, we could meet after class at the end of the day. You and me."

Thirty minutes later, still no answer.

CHAPTER 9 - EM

MY HEART'S NO longer in my chest. It jumped out as soon as I saw Jen and Nick in the hallways and went to hide because it's tired of hurting all the time. And why did I wait for them? Why did I do that to myself? When she left his room, not long after, they were hugging and it looked like they were kissing and then I don't know because I turned around so fast my head was spinning.

It's been eight months. In eight months, I should have put him behind me. I should have gotten over him. But how are you supposed to get over your first love? And over your best friend?

We still spend too much time together for me to get over him. My brain knows I can't ask him for anything, he doesn't owe me anything at this stage. He probably still believes I'm going out with that guy Andrew. But still…why Jen?

I struggle to keep the tears inside. I thought he wasn't with Jen. I thought Jen and he were over. I hide under my pillows.

And that text he sent me more than an hour ago? Like we're back to normal, like we're back to last spring as if nothing ever happened, like he never broke my heart?

I want to scream. Or cry. Or do both.

Maybe he's already sleeping—it's getting late. But I can't keep staring at his text without answering.

Em. *You don't need to wake me up tomorrow. I'll be fine.*

Nick. *Are you sure?* He types back right away as if he'd been waiting by the phone.

I'm perfectly sure.

"Goodnight," Nata says. She hasn't noticed how distraught I am, but then again, I've become super good at hiding all emotions.

"Goodnight," I reply.

She turns off her light but her breathing isn't even—she's probably thinking about the audition in two days. And that's what I should be thinking of too.

I've worked too hard to fuck it up. Too hard to let myself go. I need to nail this audition. Because if I don't, then what?

"Nata," I whisper, but she doesn't answer. Maybe she already put her iPod on. Whenever she can't sleep, she listens to Chopin. She swears it helps her fall asleep like a baby.

I, on the other hand, will turn and turn and turn.

I stare at the cracks in the ceiling, counting them. If it's an even number of cracks, I'll get the main part. If it's an uneven number, I won't.

ALWAYS SECOND BEST

I'll be second best.

I squint. There are twenty cracks, or is twenty-one? Is the last one a smudge or a crack?

I shake my head. This is not helping. I edge toward the light, and nervously check my hair for split ends. There's no noise in the hallways, no laughs, no trying to sneak out and fool the hall monitors. Is everyone sleeping? Can anyone really sleep so close to the audition?

I roll on my side and check underneath me to see if Nata's sleeping. Her eyes are closed, so she must be trying to.

And I should do the same

I never asked Nata what happened at that New Year's Eve party. The one everyone was talking about, the one where based on Jen's rumor mill, Nick and Nata made out and more. I didn't believe it then, and I still don't believe it now. It was right after I told Nick I was dating nonexistent Andrew and I know I'd hurt him, but what did he want? For me to wait? Fine, I didn't have anyone, I wasn't seeing anyone, but I could have been.

I'm sure Nick flirted with her. I'm sure Nick may have tried to kiss her, but I know he didn't. And I know because Kayode told me the truth of what happened that night, how Nick was depressed and drank too much and danced like a crazy man and held on to Nata as if she could have answers to his questions. But they didn't kiss. They didn't do anything. And Jen is poison.

Why did I decide to go see him anyways?

What is he going to tell me?

He's going to say he's sorry, and even if he says he wants to try again, what do I tell him? "Yes, sure, sorry it didn't work out with all those other girls." I toss to the other side and hug the pink blanket my birth mother had wrapped me in.

After I send the letter, I'll have to make my peace with whatever she decides. I can't force her to connect with me—if I make it to the top, I'll send her an invitation and that will be my last attempt at connecting. Dad said she wanted to sell me to the highest bidder, but after not finding anything about her having money issues, I'm not sure I believe him. He's lied to me before. Or maybe I just don't want to believe my own mother was ready to put me up for auction.

I toss around again and then take my phone in the built-in shelf inside the bed. And I do something I swore I'd stop doing: I scroll down past the pictures of ballet, and the pictures of winter, and the pictures of our big family Christmas tradition, and the pictures of Roberto and Giovanni together at Halloween, and I stop on the one Nick and I took at the Fourth of July. I must have been quite gone already, and I've only discovered that pic a few weeks ago.

He's got his arms wrapped around me, like he's not only holding me but also supporting me. I only have vague memories of that evening, but I remember that he kept me safe, I remember that he wiped my mouth after I threw up—ewww—and that we laughed for hours. He helped me forget the search for my birth mother at the time, while still being there for me.

I stare at our faces and then turn off the screen.

ALWAYS SECOND BEST

We're too far gone to ever get back to that happy place.

I wake up to one of his text messages, a picture of a squirrel flying in the air. "Good morning, sunshine." I can't help but smile. Back when we were twelve, we saw a squirrel in Central Park and one little boy was throwing rocks at it. The squirrel was up in the tree but I convinced myself he really wanted to go down. I had this entire story in my head that his family needed his help, wanted him to be there, and I told the boy to stop but he wouldn't—until Nick scared him away. I'm not sure if he remembers it, but I do, and seeing that squirrel is definitely making me smile.

My fingers hover over the screen. I type. I want to ask him what happened last night, I want to ask him a thousand questions.

Instead, I simply reply "thanks," and head out of the room. Natalya's already out. She's going to help me rehearse this morning, but she probably decided to get a head start.

I grab my toothbrush and my clothes—which are laid carefully on the chair and not on the floor—and slowly make my way out. I need coffee, but there's no time.

Despite the early hour, there's already a line for the girls' bathroom. The School expanded the dorms last year, but they're still working on adding a few necessities. I lean against the wall outside. My fingers tingle and I can't seem to be able to take a deep breath.

A few girls are chatting on the other side of the hallway and then a group of guys arrive. Nick is with them.

They say "hi" and most keep walking, since the guys' bathroom is past the corner on my left. But not Nick. Nick stops in his tracks. His eyes go up and down my body and I'm right back at this summer, when he had the exact same look, the look that says *I want you.* My entire face feels flushed. Hell, my entire body feels flushed.

I need to step away from him.

Note to feet: get moving. Our eyes collide. I want to say something, anything. He's waiting; it's like he's giving me the space I need, but he's clearly waiting for me to say something.

"See you," I croak and turn away from him.

And I want to slap myself.

CHAPTER 10 - NICK

THERE WAS A MOMENT. The way she looked at me in the hallways. There was something there. But I need to prove to her that I'm serious this time, that I won't hurt her. I've always known she had a crush on me. Hell, I always had a crush on her. I used to pull pranks on her all the time, but I haven't ever since she cried that one time when I pretended to drown and she frantically jumped in the water even though she was afraid to swim.

I gathered her in my arms and we floated back to the beach and then on the hot sand, I resisted the temptation to kiss her tears away. She would have been the first girl I kissed. She slapped me. Not hard, but she did, and she told me I was never allowed to scare her like that again.

I never did and I never will.

She stomps away to the bathroom and for a split second, I'm tempted to rush after her, to stop her, to ask her what's going on and then to kiss her troubles away. But it's not that easy. It's never been that easy.

So, instead, I hurry to get ready, to brush my teeth, and then I climb the old stairs to the second floor and open the door to one of the less-used rehearsal rooms.

I need to dance. I need to release the pressure, my anger, my doubts in the way I jump higher and higher, in the way I arch my entire body, in the way I turn so fast I forget my name.

One more rehearsal. Alone. Without anyone watching me. Without trying to impress my father or anyone.

For me.

It's been a while since I've danced for me.

I don't even turn the music on. I tap my foot on the wooden floor and then turn slowly, rising up, kicking one of my legs back and then I slowly put it back down. I tap my foot on the floor again, this time louder, with more strength, and I let the anger guide me.

I try to imagine myself ten years from now, travelling with a ballet company. And…I don't see it. I leap in the air—my hands curl into fists.

I land on one foot, turn around. This is the future I've worked so hard for, the future I was willing to sacrifice everything for. A ballet company, a shining rising star, the world at my feet.

And I fucking don't see it.

CHAPTER 11 - EM

THE DAY FLASHED BY. And it's one of those days that I can't remember, where nothing slows down, where I can't simply be in the moment. I'm following the motions, I'm following the crowd. And the crowd right now is in the canteen. And the crowd is blabbering, buzzing about tomorrow.

I wish everyone would shut up.

Can we all agree to pretend nothing's happening? My nerves are so frazzled I'm not sure I can eat. But I need to. I need the energy. Nick's sitting with us—and my entire body feels him, is attuned to him. I bring a small spoonful of chicken soup to my mouth and almost drop it when Jen struts our way.

I'm not feeling very welcoming right now.

But Nick glares at her and she turns back around.

"Trouble in paradise?" I mutter and I'm not sure anyone hears me, but Nick glances my way. He's about to say something but I don't want to get into it. Not a day before the audition.

I focus on Natalya, who's slowly eating her salad. "Did you hear from your friend Becca?" I ask her—anything to change the topic.

Nata shakes her head. "Nothing. I'll try again tomorrow…after." After that one moment that may change our year, our career, our life.

No pressure.

Nick rubs the back of his neck and clears his throat. "Do you want to go over the choreography with me again?"

I want to. I need to. But with Nick? Dancing? *Alone?* This has disaster written all over his abs.

I turn to Nata. "You're coming, too?" My voice sounds panicky. As if I can't handle an hour or two alone with Nick. Well, it's not that I can't. I don't want to.

Natalya takes another sip of her water. "I want to call my parents tonight, and you know my rules."

Which is code for…"You want to visualize all the movements the evening before and do one last rehearsal in the morning."

Natalya nods. "Yep. You and Nick should go. I'll see you in our room later." She finishes her cup of water and gets up. She brings her tray to the corner. Everything in the way she walks screams ballerina, screams future principal at amazing company, screams she's got this.

And then she strides away.

Traitor.

Not that she knows anything certain. She guessed, many people have guessed. I haven't confided in anyone. My brother is the only one who knows. Well, him and Giovanni and Kayode who guessed and the blanket my birth mother gave me, and maybe the diary I keep on and off. But none of them know how much it hurts to see him every single day, how much I wish I could take the entire summer back and at the same time relive each single moment.

I clear my throat. "Okay, well, then let's go."

And I try to pretend my heart doesn't skip a beat when our arms brush.

And I try to pretend that I don't want to pour my fears out to him.

Because he would understand. He always did.

CHAPTER 12 - NICK

THE DINNER CROWD is slowly moving back to the dorms; some are talking about going to Central Park until curfew to relax, but most are either planning on finding a spot to rehearse, or won't be able to sleep thinking how those few minutes might change our entire lives.

And part of me is focused on that too, but a big part is also solely concentrating on finding a way to make Em smile again and to ask her what's going on. Before, I could have been blunt about it. But now, she's harder to get through—she keeps me at a distance and maybe she doesn't even realize it, but it's there.

"Where do you want to go?" I hold the door for her.

"How about Room D on the second floor…it's so small no one ever wants to use it, but at least it's open."

"Your orders are my commands."

"Whatever," she replies, her face a blank mask. No smile. No scowl. Nothing except the dark circles under her eyes and the way her lips are pursed like she's trying very hard to not blurt out what's been bothering her. The hallways are full of people and the chatter seems to be nonstop. Some girl stares at me like I hung the moon or something. A freshman with stars in her eyes and I'm one of them. The reputation of the best dancer of school, the reputation of the one who can't settle down with only one girl. Her friend whispers something in her ear and she giggles—her face turning all red.

"This is ridiculous," Em mutters and even though she sounds annoyed, I can't help being happy she finally acknowledges me. I'd rather fight than get the silent treatment.

"What is? My popularity?" I nudge her and she hesitates between a smile and a frown.

"Maybe you should tell Chloe that you're back with Jen."

"What are you talking about?"

"I saw Jen leaving your room last night."

Fuck.

I rub the back of my neck as we climb the old stairs to the almost unused second floor rehearsal room.

"Jen wanted some help with…"

"You don't have to explain," Em says, but everything about the way she looks at me tells me she wants to know.

"She wanted some help with dancing. And then she wanted to borrow the USB of the dancing videos from the previous years. Nothing more."

"Yes, because you're well known for spending time with a girl alone and not doing anything."

She strides ahead and I swear I'm not looking at her ass, at her long legs. I'm not imagining them around my waist. She opens the door and slams it behind her.

I follow her inside, sighing. "Why wouldn't you believe me? We used to talk, we used to spend time doing nothing."

"Yes, and then we used to make out."

I raise an eyebrow. "Because now, we're actually going to talk about us making out. You've been avoiding the topic for months."

"We used to make out. We used to talk for hours too. And we don't do any of those anymore." She's advancing toward me. Her brown eyes hesitate between anger and pain and I want to reach out to her and pull her into a hug and ask her what's wrong. But she seems to be on the edge, wavering between falling and fighting. "We don't talk and right now, we're not going to talk. I'm not going to confide in you, I'm not going to cry on your shoulder. We're going to dance."

"If you need me, I'm there," I tell her and my voice is as firm as can be. "You know that. For anything. I'm there."

Her shoulders seem to release a bit of their tension, but then she snaps again. "Like you're there for Jen."

"Jen and I are not together," I repeat and then I'm close to her. Her breath hitches and she licks her lips. I don't even think she realizes she's doing it. "I know you're pissed and I'm sorry you're pissed, but I've been there for you for more than ten years. I've served as your punching bag before. I've listened to you cry and laugh and talk for hours. And you have no idea how much it kills me to see how I've hurt you, and you have no idea how I wish I'd handled things differently." My voice rises and I pace around. "You have to know, though, that despite everything that went down, I'm still there for you. And it has nothing to do with the fact I can still feel your lips on mine." I wink, trying to defuse the situation. "Come on, Em. We can't go on like this. We can't keep pretending we're fine." And now I sound desperate and maybe I am. I want another chance with her. But more than anything, I also don't want to lose her.

Em steps back and tilts her head, looking at me carefully like she does when she's trying to assess me. "If it's important, if you need someone to talk to, I'll always be there for you. But..." She takes a deep breath, almost like she wants to ground herself. "I don't want to be the one you use. That's all."

"I've never used you."

"Whatever," she replies and I know the conversation is over.

I turn the music on. Em stretches, letting her body fall on the leg she has propped up against the mirror. I get the spot next to hers and do the same. We switch legs. We look at each other in the mirror.

"Tomorrow, they want you to show them your technique—which is perfect—but also the emotions." I grab the remote control and change the music to *Sleeping Beauty*.

I stand next to her. And pull her to me. "We know your technique is amazing. Show me how you fall in love."

"W-what do you mean?"

"Aurora…at first she falls in love."

Em gulps but then she stares at me, raising an eyebrow that says, *Two can play this game, my friend.* "Yes." Her voice is breathy. And she may be winning the game I didn't even know we started just by looking at me.

"You need to let those emotions loose, your movements need to be full of passion, and your eyes need to have that passion in them too."

Em positions herself, with one arm up and the other behind her back. She angles her foot and then starts dancing. Her movements surround me, she surrounds me. One pirouette, one jump, one *pas de deux…* She's looking at me, like I'm her anchor point, like I'm the only thing that makes sense, like she's in love with me.

I want to grab her hand. I want to pull her to me. I want…so much.

But I know if I move she'll disappear back into that hole inside of herself.

So, instead I dance alongside her. An answer to her unspoken questions. A promise to her unspoken demand.

And when we stop, both out of breath, she kisses my cheek before turning away.

It may not be much, but it's a first step.

CHAPTER 13 – EM

THE MORNING OF THE audition is here. The morning that could change my entire life is here. I'm ready. I can't be any readier than this. My movements are perfect, my technique is perfect. I know I have a shot at it.

My stomach is in knots and I feel like I need to go to the bathroom even though I know I don't. Bile is shooting up my mouth and it's not a happy feeling.

I spent breakfast avoiding any discussion with anyone. My goal was to stay in the zone, but I never found the zone to begin with. I don't understand why I hate auditions this much—it's not the "oh it's good to be anxious, it gives you a nice boost of adrenaline," as Svetlana told us once, it's more the "I dread this so much, why am I even doing this to myself" feeling.

I shouldn't be this nervous. I shouldn't be this worried. I pace in the hallway waiting for Natalya to finish. Because, really, going after her makes sense.

Not. It's like there's something in the air and that something wants me to fail.

I turn around, pace again.

Only a few students are walking by. There's this idea that if you come too close to the audition room before your time, you will be doomed. It all comes from that legend that twenty years ago, a promising ballerina died while auditioning and her ghost went straight into the waiting person's body.

I don't believe in this story. And even if I did, maybe it'd be good to have someone else occupy me for a while.

"You need to breathe," Nick says and I jump. I may not believe in the story of the dead ballerina, but he still freaked me out.

"You were always so full of wisdom." I can't help but smile. And when he smiles back, I find myself analyzing which one of his smiles it is: the truly happy one, the confident one, the I'm-only-pretending smile?

He clears his throat and bows down. "I am the wise one."

"Between who and who?"

"You and me," he replies and those words imprint themselves in my mind, they wrap themselves around my heart. "You and me". "Me and you." And I'm about to burst into a pop song.

"Wise, my ass," I reply and the sound of his laugh weakens my knees.

"Are we really going to talk about your ass?" he asks and he watches me. Carefully watches me. He said the same thing to me last summer. We had a similar back and forth and we ended up kissing a few days later.

I gulp but don't avoid his gaze. He walks my way—looking every bit the part of the Prince Charming, even though he looks even better when he's wearing his jeans and his Mario Bros. shirt. I miss playing video games with him. I miss talking to him about everything and nothing. I miss pouring my heart out to him. I miss him.

I tilt my head, resisting the urge to run my fingers on his arm, to get closer to him. "I am breathing. Barely. But I am," I reply. "What time is your audition?"

"At three, but I thought I'd use the time to rehearse with the costume on." He pauses. "I also wanted to see you."

I don't say a word and he continues, hesitant. I'm not used to seeing Nick hesitate. "You're going to rock this. You're going to do amazing. Promise me something?"

"What?" I ask, keeping a safe distance between us. I can't think clearly when he's too close to me.

"Remember to feel everything. Every movement. Even if you're scared shitless."

"I'm never scared."

He shakes his head. "You're scared. But you don't need to be. Use this fear to show them who you are."

Shit. My throat tightens and I step forward, glance up at him. His hand automatically reaches for my face, cups it gently. "I feel so lost. Like if I don't get the main role, I'm going to lose everything. Everything I don't even have," I whisper and then blurt out, "I've been so lost since this summer. I feel like I lost myself." I've been working so hard toward this day and despite the many hours I clocked in, despite all the bunions and blood and sleepless nights, I'm still in the same position I was. I still don't know why my birth mother hates me. I still don't know who I am.

Nick bends down, his face so close to mine and I want to close my eyes, I want to feel his lips on mine again, his arms around me. "You're Emilia Moretti. You're the best Mario Brothers player. You're kind and you're strong. You're stubborn and you're talented. You're funny and you think you're awkward. You're sexy and you're amazing." His lips touch that spot right under my ear and I shiver at the contact. "Show them who you are," he repeats and this time, I nod.

"You got this," he says before striding away.

I'm not sure what happened but I know I'm grateful to him.

I'm grateful he's in my life. Despite everything that's happened.

The door of the audition room opens and my heart falls at my feet. I can't check my hair for split ends since it's super tight on the top of my head, so instead I nibble the skin around my nails.

The strange eerie calmness I felt with Nick is gone. Natalya steps out and then skips down the hall, almost running into me.

"You did great, didn't you? I can't believe I'm going after you. Right after the best student at school. I'm doomed!" I sigh. I'm right after Natalya and Jen is right after me. Natalya frowns so I quickly add, "I'm happy for you." I turn around, muttering, "I want to be first for once."

Natalya clears her throat. "You'll do fine," she tells me. "You're going to be amazing. If I'm threatened by anyone, it's you." And I want to believe her. I want to believe her so badly.

She squeezes my hand. "Look at me." our gazes lock. "You worked hard for this. You performed the routine perfectly yesterday. Let yourself go."

"What do you mean?"

"Stop overthinking the routine. Feel it. Feel every movement. When you dance, pretend Nick's the only one watching you."

"Nick? You really want me to fail, don't you?" I laugh—trying to hide how I feel, how she hit exactly the right spot. If Nick were watching me. If Nick were in the room, the only one in the room, I'd want to dance for him, I'd want to finally let go of everything.

"You want him to wake you up with a kiss. You want to live every moment of the kiss, you want everyone to feel the way you do. Show them how you feel!" Natalya's blue eyes bore into mine.

"Emilia," Svetlana calls my name. And everything slows down around me.

"You can do it. I mean it. Do you want me to wait for you?" Natalya asks.

I shake my head, not feeling my legs, not feeling my arms, not feeling anything at all except dread. "No. Go. I'll be fine. Thank you." I force my shoulders back and keep my head high, walking to the open door.

"*Merde!*" Natalya calls out the common luck charm of the ballet world. But I don't turn back to her.

Svetlana gives me a reassuring smile as I enter the room. "You got this," she whispers and I nod, but my muscles feel all tight and it's like I have tunnel vision. I can only see the faces of the judges, the way their eyes glance over me. They are sitting on chairs in front of the scene. They lean toward each other for a few seconds. They whisper "Natalya" several times and "fantastic" and one of them smiles as if he's discovered water in a desert. Of course, Natalya impressed them. As I knew she would. Nata is the best dancer at the school; I'm only crossing my fingers I maybe reached her level, or that some sort of miracle will happen.

I should really stop believing in fairy tales.

"Welcome, Emilia Moretti," the director of the school says, and I smile at the judges. The room feels bigger somehow today, but at the same time more oppressive. Maybe it's their eyes on me, the way they smile. The former prima ballerina of the American Ballet Company nods, but she purses her lips in an I-have-much-more-important-places-to-be or we've-seen-the-best, what's-the-point way.

I ground myself. I've been judged many times before. I won't pretend they're naked. I won't pretend they're not there. I'm going to give it my all, give it my best and show them that I'm worth it.

There's a familiar smell of wood and window cleaner. We're the first ones to audition so the room still smells as it does every morning.

Images of the summer flash back to me: how my body became one with the music, how I let my guard down, the pain I felt when my birth mother pushed me away, the happiness I felt when I was with Nick. How at ease. I hold on to those emotions instead of pushing them away like I usually do. Those emotions are my anchors.

"Are you ready?"

"Yes," I reply.

And I am.

The music invades me and as I turn into a pirouette, I let the story become who I am, I let myself becoming Sleeping Beauty.

I let myself believe once again.

CHAPTER 14 - NICK

I'VE NAILED IT. Nailed my audition. I jumped higher than I did in my last rehearsal and even though I missed one half turn in a pirouette, I've still nailed it. My first reaction is to dial Em, but she doesn't pick up. Maybe she decided to go back home. With the auditions, we don't have any classes to go to. Maybe she decided to go see her Nonna and spend time at the restaurant. Thinking about the restaurant brings back happy memories and I sigh.

My phone rings. "Hi Mom!"

"Hi honey, how are you?"

"Good," I reply.

"Your dad and I are trying a new restaurant tonight, you should come with us."

"Mom?"

"Yes?"

I shake my head. Of course she doesn't remember. But then she chuckles. "How was it?"

"What?"

"Your audition. I promised I would work on my priorities. And you are one of my main priorities." That's funny they didn't remember that when they left me alone on Christmas. Whatever.

"Dad promised the same thing to the counselor, and he still sent me an email about admission packages and how he could work his connections for me."

"You know your father. But enough about him. How was it?"

"I nailed it. I think I got the part."

"Good job, I knew you could do it. How about Em?" Mom and Em's mom used to be best friends too. Everything shifted when my dad fired Em's dad last year.

"I don't know yet."

"I've talked to Amanda today," she says and I'm surprised. I can't remember the last time she and Em's mom actually talked. "She told me the restaurant is doing well but that Dino's mom's been sick."

"Nonna had a stroke."

"I was so sorry to hear that. Why don't you bring Em home for dinner one night? She and Rob?" She's been insisting. That's already the second time in a few days she's mentioned it.

And I've entered an alternate universe, a world right out of one of my video games. "I don't think Dad would approve."

Mom's voice changes and turns more serious. "Your father and I talked about that. We've talked about a lot of things."

I stare at the collage Em did for me. And I think about what my father used to ask me. How he blackmailed me into going out with Jen last summer. I'm not quite sure he told Mom about *that.*

"That's good, Mom. I'm glad you guys are talking."

She's been much better since she came back from her spa-cation that almost lasted three months. My father doesn't want to lose her, that much is clear, and he's been doing everything she's asked: cutting down on his hours, going to couple's therapy twice a month and family therapy once a month.

"It's only the beginning," she sighs. "Anyways. Have to go, but I love you, bye." I can imagine her air-kissing the phone. We still have a long way to go to be as close as Em's family is.

My phone beeps—this time with a message. "Come meet in the rehearsal room. I need you." She hasn't texted me in what feels like forever and the picture I have for her on my phone is the one from last summer.

She doesn't need to ask me twice.

She's already there when I arrive. She's not dancing. She's not moving. She's leaning against the mirror with her eyes closed. And her hands shake a little.

"What's wrong?" I try to keep my voice even and strong, calm and reassuring, but I do sound worried and maybe a bit panicky. Em usually never lets her weaknesses be seen.

"I fucked it up. I fucked it all up." There are tears in her eyes that match the tears in her voice, and my heart hurts for her. And I don't care that Kayode would say I'm totally gone for Em. He would be right. There's nothing worse than loving someone, knowing how great you could be together, how great you are together, and sabotaging everything for a dream, for a lie.

She lets herself fall to the ground and looks up at me. "I lost myself in the moment but I messed up the third pirouette, my *fouetté* was the worst ever, and my body wasn't aligned for the arabesque. I know the only way for me to get a part is to shine with my technique, it's usually perfect. My dancing is dry but technically perfect. And today? Even my technique sucked!" She sniffles. "I'm never going to be first, am I?"

"What are you talking about?" I sit down next to her.

"I'm never going to make it to the top." She shakes her head. "I really thought that I could make it. How stupid am I?"

"You're not stupid. You're not stupid at all." I wrap my arm around her shoulder and she leans onto me.

"I'm going to get one of those stupid roles. One of the background dancers who does nothing but sway from one side to another."

"First, those roles are mainly for freshmen and you know it, second, you can't tell what role you're going to get. Sometimes, passion overshadows technique."

She snorts. "I hate it when you're being overly optimistic."

"I'm being realistic—you're feeling sorry for yourself." I stand up as her eyes widen. "Come on, let's dance."

"I left a note to Nata I was going to go rehearse, but the last thing I want to do right now is dance."

"Come on, close your eyes and forget everything else."

"You've always been good at making me forget," she whispers and then blushes so hard I'm guessing she didn't mean to say that out loud. "I-I mean…" she stutters.

"Come on, get up," I tell her again. "I double dare you." I wink and I know I got her. I turn the music up so loudly we can barely hear our own thoughts and I pull her to me. This time, we don't dance side by side, we dance together, molded to one another. We don't speak but my hands travel down her back and I pick her up from her waist. She holds on to my shoulders, stretching and extending her legs into a split, then I bring her closer to me. She stretches her arms above her head, arching her back as I spin around the room with her. She smiles but then purses her lips, probably remembering she's supposed to be mad at me and at the world.

It's been so long since this summer, it's been so long since I felt her pressed against me. I slowly get her back on the floor. And the words tumble out of my mouth. "Maybe you and I, we should try it again."

"What are you talking about?" She gasps.

"You and I. We've been on eggshells around each other. We've tried to pretend nothing happened and we're a big fucking failure at it."

"I think we're doing pretty well. Plus I'm with Andrew," she replies with her chin up. Which means at least she forgot about the audition and is ready to argue with me to no end.

"Does that guy even exist?" I retort—and I don't care if the eggshells explode.

"Does it really matter?"

"Of course, it does!"

"I wish he existed," she answers and I know. There's no one else.

"About Jen… About this summer."

Her entire posture stiffens. "I don't want to hear it!"

"We said we would only be together for the summer." In my mind, I understand why she's mad, but at the same we both agreed to those stupid rules, plus she lied about finding that Andrew guy.

Her eyes widen like I punched her in the stomach.

"Come on, listen to me. You said you wanted to focus on dancing and that's what I wanted too, but…."

She doesn't let me finish. She shouts. "You were right. You and I…we'll never work!"

"This is total BS and you know it. I was wrong." I take a deep breath. There's so much I want to tell her. "I can't stop thinking about you." Her mouth gapes open. "I want to kiss you. Tell me you don't want me to and I won't." I don't make a move. I want to give her a choice, I want to know she wants it too.

We'll figure out a way to make it work. I know I can. I know we can. She rises on her toes and I cup her face with one hand, while the other snakes around her waist. "You're driving me crazy," I tell her as she watches me—a challenge in her eyes.

When our lips meet, I'm on fire. I deepen the kiss, it's urgent and fast and everything I've wanted to do for the past eight months but didn't. It's everything I shouldn't want but can't live without.

She pulls away from me but then tugs me back to her. "You have no idea how much I've missed you," she whispers and kisses me again.

I'm going to have to tell her.

I'm going to have to stand up to my father.

But now? Now I want to enjoy the feel of her body against mine, and the way her lips taste.

CHAPTER 15 - EM

I FORGET MYSELF in his kiss, in the way his arms tighten around me, in the way my entire body wants to get even closer.

One of his hands cups the side of my face. I jump so my legs are around his waist. He's holding me and I deepen our kiss. I don't ever want to stop.

"Em." His voice is hoarse and he walks forward, my legs still around him, until my back hits the mirror.

His lips trail down my face, to my collarbone, and his hands detangle mine from his neck to bring them over my head.

I can feel him, all of him. "I've missed you," he says.

And I've missed him too. So much. My brain's screaming for me to stop, my heart's hesitating. What am I doing? What are we doing? Setting ourselves up for failure again.

"I have to go." My voice shakes. "I have to go," I repeat and Nick slowly puts me back on my feet before stepping away.

"What are you talking about?" He's almost out of breath.

"I have to go." I can't look at him, or I'll never leave.

I rush out. My feelings and my heart trailing behind.

Nata's here when I enter our room. She looks up and her eyes widen. I'm pretty sure my entire face is red and that my hair is more out of control than usual. I could talk to her, but the way my throat tightens is a clear indicator that I'm about to lose it. I blink rapidly to stop the tears from falling.

"Are you okay?" She asks and tilts her head to the side—as if wondering if she should talk to me or if she should give me some privacy.

Everything is still too raw: the auditions which I know she nailed while I failed, the wonderful and yet oh so confusing making-out session with Nick.

So I lie. "Totally fine." My shrug is a pitiful attempt to pretend that my words are true. I force my lips into a small smile. "Tired, that's all. What time are you leaving tomorrow?"

"Super early, I have a morning flight."

"I'm tired, I'll turn in early too." I yawn as if to prove my point. I pick up my shower bag, my bright blue towel and my pj's. My eyes focus on the ballerina posters she has on her side of the room. "Sometimes, I wonder if I'm cut out for all of this." I blurt out. "I'm happier in the restaurant with my Nonna than I am here. But I'm good, right?"

"You're amazing," Nata replies, tugging on her necklace. She looks directly at me. "But dancing should make you happy."

"I don't know what makes me happy." My fake laugh is dry, and I blow a strand of hair away from my face. "Listen to me, having a pity party. I'll be back."

And I close the door behind me. Maybe, I should talk to Nata, ask her what she thinks. Maybe we could for once forget everything that's dancing and simply talk and talk and talk all night. Maybe Nata needs the distraction too. She seems preoccupied. I have a feeling that not asking me what bothers me is a way to protect herself and her feelings. She hates asking for help, and she hates appearing vulnerable but I know the situation with her parents—how they fight all the time—has been on her mind.

I'll ask her how she's doing. I'll make sure she knows I'm there for her, that showing when she's hurt

ALWAYS SECOND BEST

is not making her weaker. But first, I need to get myself back together.

When I come back after taking a long shower, she's already asleep.

CHAPTER 16 – NICK

"EM!" I CALL OUT. But I don't run after her. She needs her space and I need time to become rational. Right now, I'd beg her and promise her the world. Her eyes were full of worries, uncertainties, almost panic. And once more I want to kick past-Nick in the balls.

Of course, she's worried. Of course, she wonders what the hell we're doing. Of course, she's not sure.

I breathe in deeply.

I'll call her, I'll talk to her tonight or tomorrow. We're going to figure this out together.

And I'm going to go home, and face my father.

No matter what the outcome of this audition is, no matter what Emilia decides, no matter what the next few weeks might be, I can't simply ignore the past and not confront him.

It's time.

ALWAYS SECOND BEST

CHAPTER 17 - EM

THERE'S SOMETHING SOOTHING about having my hands in ground meat—making *polpette*. Nonna always makes sure the restaurant serves those Italian meatballs at least once a week and then she usually goes table to table to explain what *polpette* are and how different from meatballs they are. I form a small round with my fingers. During the entire weekend, my mind replayed the audition, the kiss with Nick, the way I ran out after a make-out session that was well deserving of the Guinness Record for hotness.

He tried to call me. Five times. He called Roberto asking him if I'm doing okay.

And I am. But I'm so scared of getting hurt again. So scared of putting my heart out there only to hear him tell me that we need to stop, that he needs to focus on being the best, that we can try it out for a few weeks, see how it goes.

I can't do that to myself again. Live, love and learn. Or in this case: live, love, cry every night for two weeks, then pretend you don't know your own best friend, then pretend you're fine with him dating other people, and then almost pull yourself back up.

But the way his arms felt around me, the way his lips tasted, the way his kiss felt like a promise of more.

I've always dreamed Nick would be my first— way before I even tasted his lips. Now? I've been thinking I might need to stay a virgin all my life if I can't have him.

ALWAYS SECOND BEST

I've kissed two guys before Nick: Sloppy McSloppy (me, not him) who never called me again and too-good-to-be-true asshole when I started at the School of Performing Arts. He ended up dropping out. He was definitely too good to be true and also had a bit of an issue with coke. Not Diet Coke. I wash my hands.

"You're either in love or you're having a stroke," Nonna says and chuckles.

"That's so not funny," I reply and she hugs me.

"If I can't laugh about it, who else will?" she replies.

"No one. You shouldn't be laughing about it and no one should be laughing about it."

"I'd rather spend my last good years, or months or weeks, laughing at death coming than being afraid to look at it in the eyes, Bellisima." she checks on the boiling *polpette*. "Have you eaten?"

"Not yet," I reply. "They're not going to be ready for another thirty minutes or so."

"Why don't you sit down with me and then we'll eat," she says and we settle at a table she has set on the side of the kitchen.

She puts her hand on mine. "Loving is scary. And sometimes getting hurt is worth it. I was hurt when your Poppa passed away. I was hurt when I lost your aunt and she was so little. But I don't regret those loves because they didn't mean to hurt me. I didn't go into those relationships thinking how bad they were for me, but rather how good they made me feel." She catches her breath. "If you're afraid to get hurt, there's a good chance he's worth you giving him a chance. But if you know you're going to get hurt, for no good reason, he's not worth your time, and certainly not worth your love."

"What if I already got hurt?"

"Maybe you both weren't ready." She leans forward. "You were not the only one who got hurt this summer, Bellisima. Nicholas did too."

My eyes widen and she chuckles. "I'm old but I'm not blind. Now, tell me more about the recipe you used for the *polpette*."

I tell her about mixing her recipe with one I found online, how I added a few herbs. And for the next thirty minutes, we talk about food and how Nonna and Poppa opened their restaurant almost forty years ago.

"Dinner is ready. And you need to eat." She stands up and hands me a plate. "I don't want you to become one of those ballerinas I've seen on the Lifetime movies I watch. Or like those dancers you told me about. No art is worth your sacrifice."

I take the plate, sit down in front of her. "How do you know someone is right for you, Nonna?" I clear my throat. "How did *you* know? It seems like you hit the jackpot twice, both with Poppa and with Mr. Edwards."

She chuckles. "You only know us as Nonna and Poppa, Bellisima. We didn't show you the struggles, the fights. I never told you about that one time we almost split up. After years of courting and passion and everything else in between, we didn't know anymore. Love is easy and love is hard. Love can bring tears to your eyes and joy in your heart. But you should know if the person is worth the risk, worth the pain. You have to be partners and lovers and…"

She wipes away a tear. "Every day I miss your grandfather. Every day I wish I could talk to him and joke with him. He was the great love of my life. Ben— Mr. Edwards—is wonderful and it's a different kind of love."

"Poppa and you almost split up?"

"After he got back from the war, it was difficult. But I would never take a day away from the days I had with him. The hard ones made the easy ones even easier. And we learned from one another. We grew together." She sips on her daily glass of red wine. "You can believe in fairy tales, Bellisima, but know that you need to make it happen." She twirls her food with her fork on her plate. "Now eat before it gets cold. I promised your mother I would push you out of here by five p.m. so you get back to school before it gets dark again."

I don't bother to argue with her. Mom wants her to rest, and she wants to check on her—that's why I need to leave by five. Nonna winks at me while eating and I wonder if maybe she's on to the secret and simply lets it go because she loves us.

At five p.m. sharp, I leave the restaurant. The wind's blowing and the snow can't stop falling. My mind's still buzzing from Nonna's advice—and this time, when Nick calls, I pick up.

"I'm sorry I've been ignoring you," I tell him.

"And I'm sorry I've been a jerk. I've got lots of explaining to do."

"I need to ask. Do you want to see where we're going? Where we can go?" My heart's at my feet, waiting for his answer. Because what if he says no.

"I want to say yes."

"But?" Fear bubbles within me. Nonna is right I won't put myself in a situation where I know I'll get hurt because he doesn't want to stand up to his dad, or because he's afraid I'm going to hurt his chances at a career. Been there, done that.

"But I want to tell you something. Tonight— when I'm back. I might be late. But wait for me, okay?"

"And then?"

"And then you decide."

"You do realize I might not be first, right? That I most likely will not get the role, which means according to your career plan, I might be a distraction."

"Not being with you ends up being more of a distraction."

"Oh." I don't know what else to say.

"Try not to fall asleep like you sometimes do right at eight thirty p.m."

"I work hard, I'm tired."

He chuckles. "I can't wait to see you."

I hurry all the way to school.

When I get back into my room, Natalya hasn't gotten back yet. Her flight back to New York from Maine might have been delayed. With all the snow falling down, that wouldn't be surprising.

I'm feeling a bit calmer.

The weekend spent at Nonna's did help to alleviate some of my stress, some of my worries about the results. If I get one of the main roles I'll be happy, I just don't want to be dancing in the back this year. And I can't wait to see Nick. I can't wait to hear what he has to say. I can't wait to see if we can move past the hurt and the awkwardness.

I open the drawer and pull out the blanket I was wrapped in when my father bought me.

He bought me. This is still hard to swallow—no matter how many sessions we're doing with our family counselor. The blanket has a pink ballerina on it with the words "I love to dance."

And I know, deep inside, that even if I can mend my relationship with Nick, a part of me still needs to prove to my birth mother she was wrong to slam the door on me, to prove to her that she can be proud of me, to prove to her that I deserve her love.

If she doesn't reply to my letter, I'll call her. I'll see her. I only want one more chance.

CHAPTER 18 - NICK

"NICK!" MY FATHER CALLS ME from the living room. He and Mom have decided they needed to spend at least thirty minutes together each night, without any distractions, meaning he can't read his *Wall Street Journal* or his BlackBerry, and Mom can't be thinking about something else.

They talk.

Sometimes, they fight.

I even saw them kiss one time.

They make me believe that maybe they'll make it work.

"Nick!" he calls again and he doesn't sound happy. At. All.

I grab my bag and head his way. "Coming."

I poke my head inside. Dad's sitting on the leather couch with a martini in his hand and his iPad in his hand. Mom's nowhere to be seen. Weird.

"I'd like you to take Liz to a charity event next week."

ALWAYS SECOND BEST

News travel fast in the business world. Maybe it is going to be on a Bloomberg ticker on TV tonight. "Son of business mogul refuses to be used any longer."

I clear my throat and bore my eyes into my father's. "I'm not going to go out with Liz."

"And why is that?"

"Because I don't want to."

"You sound like a five-year-old."

"And you sound like you haven't heard me. I'm not going out with her. This is over."

My father stands up and we're facing one another, like I should have done years ago. But I'm a coward—it's much easier to do so now that my last year at the School is paid and I've learned one or two things along the way.

"I can ruin your career."

"And I can ruin yours," I reply. "If people knew you've been blackmailing me to go out with girls, who do you think is going to see his stocks plummet? You or me?"

"You have no idea what you're talking about." But he's not as tall as he used to be, or as he seemed. He's not as scary anymore either.

"I'm no longer playing your little game. You're lucky I haven't told Mom—I don't think she'd be too pleased."

"Leave your mom out of this. Especially right now."

"Then you leave me out of it too! I'm almost eighteen."

"Like it changes anything. It doesn't. If you wanted to leave you'd already have done it, and you didn't complain before this summer. It's all about Em, isn't it?"

"Leave Em out of this."

"You're so clueless. You are so clueless. I told you you needed to stay away from the Moretti family. You need to stay away from them!"

"Emilia's dad was here two weeks ago."

"He and I have things to discuss."

"Why can't you be more like him?"

My father steps back but then shakes his head. "You really don't understand anything. Why do you think I fired him?"

"Because he didn't want to play dirty."

"Because he played dirty."

"He played dirty?" I repeat, not believing one word of my world-class business-cheating dad. He's the one who managed to sell stocks that were barely legal to a bunch of retired people.

He's one scandal away from jail.

"Believe me or don't believe me, it doesn't matter. What matters is that I don't want you to hang out with Emilia. I don't want you to hang out with Roberto. I don't want you to hang out at their restaurant. You don't want to help me any longer? Fine. But you'd better listen to me on this."

"Why?"

"Because I said so."

"It doesn't make any sense." I cross my arms over my chest and stare at him, not backing down, when he frowns and when he sighs loudly.

"Are you even listening to what I'm saying?" Dad leans against his desk. "Are you listening to any words I'm saying?"

"Are you listening? You screwed up, Dad. On so many levels. And for what?"

"I've been protecting this family. I've done my best to protect this family."

I step forward. I'm in his face now, but I'm not going to raise my voice. The voice of steel is what I'm going to use. "You almost completely lost this family. Mom wanted to leave you. I spent more time with the Morettis than here. All you cared about was your business. At least with the Morettis…"

He raises his hands. "Stop talking about what you don't know."

"Again, I know. I've spent holidays with them. I've spent Sundays and evenings and dinner with them." Not counting the times that Em's dad made it clear I was no longer as welcome and that he was solely tolerating me because of his family.

"And this has to stop. You need to let go of the Morettis. Concentrate on what you call a career. Whatever that actually is."

"You're not giving me any reasons to let go," I push him.

"I don't need to give you reasons. I'm your father."

"When that's convenient for you." I shrug—knowing very well how much he's annoyed when I do that. He thinks I'm being careless when I'm really trying to protect myself.

"You don't know the half of what I've done."

"I know you lied. I know you manipulated me. I know you used me. I know you made Mom cry and you made me wish I was adopted."

His face pales and he curls his hands into fists. "You need to calm down, Nick."

I chuckle. "Why? You can't fire me. And I'm not scared of you."

He inhales deeply and exhales loudly. "I'm going to say it one last time: stay away from them. Is it so hard to understand?"

"If you're not giving me any more reasons than this, then yes, it's pretty hard to understand."

"You want reasons? I'll give you reasons!" My father's shouting now. He never shouts. His calmness is his trademark, his signature. "The entire story about Em's adoption is bogus, what he said about Claire trying to sell her, it's bullshit. And you know what else? Em's father is the one who falsified the documents for those stocks that almost got me fired. He's got a lot of other problems." He stares at his hands for a second before staring at me again. "I don't want you hanging out around them. You deserve so much better than them, and not because they no longer have any money. When Dino cheated those people from their pension, he lost all my respect."

My mouth drops open.

"What are you talking about?" I say. "What are you saying?"

"I'm saying that there are always several sides to a story, and when it comes to Em's adoption, you two need to leave it alone. I'm saying that Emilia's father went down a dark path last year, and that's why I had to fire him. Amanda doesn't know about it. No one except your mom and I know about it."

"Why wouldn't you say anything about Em's adoption? Why didn't you tell me?"

"Because it's not my place to tell," he replies, but my eyes bore into his. I'm not backing down.

"Dad." I only say this one word, and he looks at me for a few seconds before letting himself fall on his leather chair.

"Fine. Because it's not my place to tell and because Dino and I agreed about certain things when I helped him with the paperwork. Back then, he may have helped me gain a bit more money on a business deal thanks to insider information he gathered during a meeting. But that was back then. I've never used the system again."

"I don't believe you. You have no heart. No fucking heart. Em's been dealing with thinking her mom tried to sell her, she's been trying so hard to find ways to impress her birth mother, to impress her parents, to impress me." My voice breaks on the last word and I clear my throat. "You guys are killing me. Is it all games for you? Is it all about money?"

My father slouches. Gone is the elegance and the imposing attitude; he looks his age and he looks tired. "It used to be all about money, until your mother gave me an ultimatum. I'm really trying, Nick. But I can't accept you compromising yourself with that family. Not when everything I worked so hard for is on the line. Not when our lives are on the line."

"Me seeing Em or not won't change anything."

"It will change everything. She's going to hold you back. Em's father will not let her date you."

"Why?"

"Because he doesn't want her to find out what I told you."

"She needs to know. She's been working so hard on everything."

"He's not going to let that happen. And I'm not either. You can call me an asshole or whatever you want, but I'm not letting you waste your time and energy on her. She's not for you. Their family is drowning in debt, they're drowning in their problems. Em's father's been trying to get back to our firm, but I can't let that happen. And I won't let him use you."

"Not everyone wants money. Not everyone dreams about being you."

"Dino does! You have no idea. And you won't get down to that level. You need to date someone from our circles. What's going to happen when you realize your dancing isn't taking you anywhere? When you realize you're only trying to defy me? Trust me, Nicholas, defying your own father only works for that long. I should know." He glances at the family pictures on the chimney. "Don't make the same mistakes I have, Nicholas. Learn through me."

"Whatever. You married Mom. And you had no money compared to her. None."

"And are we happy?" He coughs. "And it's different. I came from a well-off family. Sure our fortune wasn't as big as your mom's, but we were still high society and I had a good degree, I was going somewhere. Plus don't even think about marriage now, son. You're only seventeen. You need to explore your options."

"What are you going to do if I decide to date Em?"

"Do you know who's paying for Em's dance school right now?"

"Em's parents," I reply, wincing, knowing where he's heading with this, not believing he would put his threat into actions.

"No. I am."

"You wouldn't."

"Would you bet on it though?"

I look at him, really look at him. And despite the anger bubbling within me, I remember him begging my mother to not leave him, I remember him at a charity auction three years ago giving his coat and his shoes to a homeless person the organization didn't want to let in because he didn't look the part for the TV crews who were there, I remember him laughing with me at one of my birthday parties. I was feeling sick and he stayed with me—actually missing a day of work. When did everything change? When did he become so hardened that he can't see himself anymore?

He sighs. "Nicholas, would you bet on it?"

I don't want to bet on Em. There's no way I would risk Em's future. But he doesn't have to know that I'm bluffing. He doesn't need to know I'm lying to his face right now, because if he ends up even remotely appearing to be removing the money plug, I'll do whatever he says. I will. For her.

But I need to believe he won't do that to Emilia, because there's no way in hell my father has turned into this heartless monster. He's an ass, he doesn't understand me, he uses me, but he can't be that mean.

"Nicholas?" His voice is strong and sure, but a part of me knows he's lying. Maybe it's in the way his eyes dart from mine to the door, or maybe in the way he rubbed the back of his neck—once.

I take a leap of faith. "I would." And I cross my fingers he doesn't see me cringe.

He sighs. "I used to be good at bluffing, but not anymore apparently. I would have cut your funds, without blinking. But not Emilia's. She's innocent in all that." He smiles and ruffles my hair like he used to and for a split second I imagine us getting along again, I imagine us having a semblance of a life. But then he turns serious once more. "You're going to do as you please. But let me warn you, Dino is not going to be happy."

"That's not his choice either." My voice is firm and when I leave the house, I feel five thousand feet taller.

CHAPTER 19 - EM

I TRY VERY hard to keep my eyes open: I do stretches, I listen to the eighties playlist on Pandora. That playlist always reminds me of the good times I did have last summer, how I danced to mom's Madonna's collection. I try to come up with a new dessert recipe for Nonna's restaurant. Something with chocolate. Always chocolate.

Every few seconds, I check my phone, I check the split ends of my hair, I check Nata's side as if she'd magically appear. Her plane must have been canceled. She's running late and she must be freaking out. I text her but no answer.

My fingers itch to dial Nick's phone but I don't want to do it. I don't want to be the one reaching out to him. Again.

Where is he?

I try to watch something online, but can't concentrate.

And then a knock at my door.

"Nick?" I say, but Jen opens the door.

"What do you want?" I can't even use my I'm-nice tone with her.

"I wanted to talk to Natalya, she's not picking up her phone."

"Since when do you talk to Nata? I didn't even know you had her phone number." I narrow my eyes at her—what game is she playing now?

"Well, I guess you don't know everything. Natalya was supposed to help me with something. Anyways…have you heard from her?" She crosses her arms over her chest.

"I'm sure her flight's having some delays—she's not back yet."

Jen stretches her neck as if to check if I'm lying or not "I heard you really impressed the jury at the audition." She doesn't sound all that surprised which is almost hard to believe.

"I'm sure we all did," I reply. I so don't want to get into a talk with her. Not when Nick's supposed to be here. Not when I'm supposed to finally have the talk with him. Not when I believe maybe, just maybe, we finally have a chance again.

There's a commotion in the hallways, and Nick's laugh booms. He's talking to his roommate, something about coming back later tonight.

Jen puts her hand on her hip. "He's looking good tonight. I think you saw us the other day?"

"You mean when he helped you with your choreography and you tried to make out with him? Yes, I saw that. I don't understand why you keep holding on."

"Why do you?"

ALWAYS SECOND BEST

Fair question. "Because when we were fourteen and Matt dumped me in front of the entire class for being a sloppy kisser, I cried for hours. Nick spread the rumor that we were dating and that he was the reason I broke up with Matt." I smile, remembering. "Because, a few weeks later, he convinced Roberto to let me play with them, when I had a fight with my best friend and no one to hang out with. Because, two years ago, we talked all night and laughed all day while we were at the Hamptons."

She pales. Nick's almost at my door and he frowns when he sees her, but I shrug and stare at her. "Because last summer was the best and worst summer of my life, and I don't want to be afraid anymore."

Jen snickers. "Pretty nice speech. But don't forget something: Nick is reaching for the stars. You don't want to be holding him back." She turns on her heels and I could almost believe what I said didn't upset her, if I didn't notice the way her shoulders slouched. Jen never ever slouches. That's not her style. Despite everything that's happened and how bitchy she's been, a part of me really does feel sorry for her. Nonna says there are two categories of mean people: the ones who find joy in spreading negativity, and the ones that feel destroyed by it but who don't know how to change. I want to believe Jen's in the second category.

I stay by the door, and my eyes can't stray from Nick's. He's still wearing his jacket and his boots are dripping wet. He's got his hat on and I didn't think I could melt until now.

He has a half smile on and as soon as he's in front of me, I pull him inside my room, away from the

curious glances. Curfew is in two hours, and if one of the teacher assistants or residential hall assistants makes the rounds and see him there, he could get in lots of trouble.

"You're cold," he tells me as he kisses the top of my nose.

"You're bringing snow in," I whisper even though there's no one else in the room. It's only the two of us.

"I have so many things to tell you. So many things," he says. "I can't kiss you before I tell you any of them."

My heart squeezes. "Let me ask you three questions, and then we'll see if we do the kissing before or after the talking."

He chuckles. "So pragmatic."

"One of us has to be. First question: do you want to kiss me?"

"You know I do."

"Second question: do you want to be with me?"

"You know I do."

"Third question: do you want to give us a real chance? No bullshit?"

"You know I do."

My heart is so full I'm not sure it's not going to explode. I pull him to me, not caring about the cold anymore, and this time when our lips meet there's so much passion I'm surprised I'm not combusting.

There's no hesitation. One of his hands presses against the small of my back, and his lips trail down to that spot on my neck he knows oh so well. "I've missed you," he says. "I've missed you so much."

ALWAYS SECOND BEST

I tilt my head to give him better access, and I want to feel him closer. Oh so much closer.

But a knock at my door stops us cold.

"If it's Jen again, I'm going to kill her."

"We still need to talk," Nick whispers.

"Emilia. Emilia, it's Svetlana. Are you there?"

"What is she doing here?" I shake my head. "Just a second."

"If you're worried about Nick being in there with you, curfew hasn't started yet so you're fine." I open the door.

"We need to talk, sweetie."

Svetlana's usually very well dressed, very well put together, but right now she's in sweatpants and a large NYC sweatshirt. She's not wearing her contacts, but big glasses instead, and her dark hair kind of sticks out in different places. A fist of fear tightens my chest.

Svetlana blinks her eyes rapidly as if she's trying not to cry. "Natalya had an accident. Her father's dead and she's in a coma."

CHAPTER 20 - NICK

FUCK.

I wrap an arm around Em, who's shaking. I don't know if it's from the cold I brought in or the news about Natalya.

Em turns her head to me, her eyes wide and her voice small. "It doesn't make any sense. Nata's fine." She turns back to Svetlana. "Nata has to be fine." There are tears in her voice and I feel numb. I saw Nata on Friday. We all knew she had the best chance at getting the main part of the showcase. We all knew she was going to be discovered—if she hadn't been already—and might have even started her career earlier than us. We all knew Nata's meant for dancing, that's what she breathes and bleeds.

Svetlana touches my hand quickly before pulling Emilia into a hug. She's crying too now and her voice shakes. "It was a bad accident. Her uncle called us. Her father didn't make it and she's got some pretty bad fractures and they don't know at this stage if she'll be able to walk again, let alone dance."

Emilia holds on to Svetlana for a few seconds without a word. "What can I do?" she asks. "I'm sure there's something we can do. She loved her father so much. I don't understand. It doesn't make sense," she says again and leans into me. Emilia feels so much. For everyone. She hates showing it, but she does. Even when we were little, she fought for the ones people were making fun of, she made Valentine's cards for the kid everyone shunned away. And right now, I'm sure she's also thinking about her own grandmother and how almost losing her affected her. She doesn't want that for Nata.

"The School will organize something. I wanted to be the one to tell you before the school assembly tomorrow."

"Why are we still having the school assembly?"

"Because we should find out more about Natalya's condition tomorrow and we'll make our decision then."

"The show really does go on," I say and it leaves a bitter taste in my mouth. "You have to give Nata a chance."

"Her injuries are bad, as I said."

"If she can't dance, she'll have nothing to live for," Em whispers. "Nothing." I squeeze her hand.

"I know," Svetlana replies, and I remember how Svetlana also knows Nata's mother and how protective she's been of her. She wouldn't do anything that would harm her, unless she really had to. It wasn't her decision. It must come from higher up.

Those people have the final say.

Svetlana wipes away her tears. "She's strong. Natalya's strong and we don't know what might happen. Maybe the doctors are wrong and she'll be able to recover quickly." She shakes her head. "It really puts everything in perspective," she mutters and then gives Em another hug. This time, she doesn't linger. It's like she's trying to recover and to put some distance between her and the events, like it hits too close to home almost.

"Please, don't tell anyone yet. I really wanted you to know first, but…" She touches her watch, looking at it before glancing back up. "But some didn't agree that you should have preferential treatment."

"Preferential?" I struggle with the words. That's so much bullshit.

"Anyways, I'll see you both tomorrow." her eyes dart from me to Em a few times. "You know that after curfew you're not supposed to be in the same room, right?" She says it slowly as if she's making sure we understand.

"We know," I reply. Svetlana nods and leaves us alone.

I slowly cup Em's face in my hands, caressing her cheek with my thumb.

"I can't believe it," she says. "I'm here worried about you and me, about how to tell you I want to be with you, about how to tell you I don't want to be temporary…while Natalya's laying in a hospital bed. Her father's dead!" Her eyes are wide and her voice sounds panicky. I don't know what to do. There's so much I need to tell her, so much I need to share with her. I could wait, I could wait for a better moment, I

could wait for a time where she's not already struggling, but there's a feeling inside of me that pushes me to tell her now.

I can't start our relationship by omitting the truth. I rub the back of my neck and I feel her tensing against me.

"What's wrong?" she asks.

"What?" I reply.

"You're worried about something. You always get that look when you're about to say something that you think might hurt me." She sounds tired, as if the news about Natalya took everything out of her.

"Why don't you sit?"

She raises one eyebrow—I taught her that move, but I hate it when she pulls it on me. "Why don't you simply tell me what's going on?"

"It's my dad. I have lots to tell you. A lot. But he said something tonight about your birth mother."

"About Claire?"

"He said there's much more to the story, that you don't know everything." I keep the details about her dad to myself—I'm still not quite sure if Daddy Dearest told the truth about that. Their business venture seems to be a nest of snakes...one trying to outdo the other. She doesn't say a word. "Em?"

"What do you mean?"

"He said there was more to the story than what we know. Apparently, your mom didn't try to sell you like your father said. Apparently, it's a lie. "

Em blinks rapidly, but silent tears still fall down her face. I pull her back to me. She still hasn't said a word and that's freaking me out. Between

Natalya, the auditions and this, I'm not sure how she feels.

She buries her face in the crook of my neck, breathing in and out slowly, trying to calm down. After a few seconds, she leans back and looks at me. "What more? What else is there? Can it be any worse? Do you know how I felt when Claire pushed me away last summer?"

I hug her tighter—hoping my arms around her can soothe her, hoping I can protect her from the sadness I hear in her voice, hoping that together we can be stronger.

She tilts her head back and looks into my eyes. "I felt like I didn't matter. Like I was the biggest mistake in her life. Like she hated me." She swallows. "I've done enough research to know that some birth mothers really want nothing to do with their kids, but that look she gave me—as if I stole everything from her—it killed me. In a way, hearing there's more to the story is either a relief because maybe there are more reasons behind her attitude, or it's scary because it could be even worse." She lets herself fall on the bed and pulls me next to her. "And how am I going to know? She's not talking to me. Your father isn't really telling us anything. And I don't know how to ask questions to my father anymore either. He's withdrawn so much since this summer. Did Roberto tell you?"

"What?"

"My dad's been gone a lot. At night. He's a financial advisor for a small firm—he's no longer having late-night meetings with big mergers and whatever else they were doing."

"Maybe it is work-related. Does he talked about his job a lot?"

"He doesn't, and that really only started since my Nonna had a stroke. I don't know what's going on."

Rob didn't tell me shit, and I can't believe Em has also been mum about it. "Why didn't you tell me?"

"Because we spent a month almost not talking, three months pretending to talk and the rest kind of existing next to one another since last summer. I didn't know how to talk to you anymore."

"And now?"

"Just because I didn't know how to talk to you, didn't mean I didn't want to…"she whispers. "When my Nonna had a stroke, you were the first person I wanted to call."

"You did call me."

"I know, and you were there for me. You listened and you let me cry and you didn't tell me everything was going to be okay because we didn't know that."

"And the next day you ignored me."

"I didn't know how to be around you."

I link my fingers with hers. "I have so much more to tell you, so much more to explain."

She rests her head on my shoulders. "But not right now." She sounds tired and so sad.

"Not right now."

And we stay in each other's arms without a word, without kissing, without doing anything but pulling strength from one another until curfew.

CHAPTER 21 - EM

NICK MAY HAVE LEFT my room right on time for curfew, but that didn't mean we stopped talking—we chatted almost the entire night. It was like trying to make up for the months where we kept each other an arabesque away.

I think I wasn't ready to let go back then—I was too distraught by the discovery that my birth mother didn't want anything to do with me. He was too consumed by whatever it was... I want to know and I want to hear his explanations, but I'm also not stupid: we hurt one another last summer. I got my heart stomped on, but I'm pretty sure pushing me away wasn't easy for him either.

But tonight it wasn't about us. It wasn't about our relationship, or about Claire Carter and all the lies. Tonight it was about Natalya and her accident and what happened, and why we can't find anything concrete. Only a small article so far about the accident—and really only about her father passing

away. My chest constricts and again, taking a full deep breath seems impossible.

I keep on looking at her side of the room, I keep on wondering how she's feeling and how she's doing and how to help her.

I get ready more slowly than usual. I don't want to answer questions about Natalya's absence before the assembly.

I don't want to see the looks of pity people will have. Because she's not there. Because she's not going to get the role everyone knows should be hers.

I keep my eyes trained to the floor on my way to breakfast, but Jen stops me. "Have you heard?" There's no triumph in her voice, only fear and sadness. No pity either. Jen and Natalya were never close—but Jen did talk once or twice to Natalya about them rehearsing together. She made it seem like she could help Nata, while clearly she would have been the one to learn something. Maybe, that's what they were supposed to do last night.

"I've heard and I'm guessing the entire school's heard."

"This sucks. This fucking sucks," she says and my eyes widen. Jen never swears. Never, ever.

"I know," I reply.

"We should do something. We should ask them to postpone the results of the audition until they know for sure how she's doing, if maybe she'll be able to join again."

"Why would you do that?" I can't help but ask.

"Because that's her life. Because that's my life. Because if that happened to me, I don't know what I'd do." She tilts her head to the side, as if she's assessing me. "You know why I sometimes hate you?"

"Sometimes?"

Jen shakes her head. "It has nothing to do with Nick. It has nothing to do with him," she repeats when I make a face. "It's about you. It's about how you're dancing for all the wrong reasons."

"Huh?"

"We've been in the same school for years. I've seen you dance. I've seen you rehearse. You're amazing, and you don't even care. You don't feel all the emotions when you're arching your arms, or when the music is supposed to transport you. You don't dance with your heart, and that's killing me because I'd die to have your technique."

I think someone tilted the universe off its axle. I have to call Roberto and ask him if some natural phenomenon happened that made this moment possible.

"I love dancing."

Jen purses her lips. "You don't understand it, do you? I live for dancing. Like Natalya. You don't." She turns away before I can reply, sitting down alone at a table. She's wrong. She can't be right. I love dancing. I really do. It's what I do. It's who I am. Because if she's right, then what the hell am I doing?

⁂

The entire student body population knew about Natalya's car accident before the general assembly. People whisper, commiserate; some, however, only wonder what's going to happen to the showcase.

ALWAYS SECOND BEST

Everyone believes Jen will get the role, but one girl approached me to tell me she hopes it's me.

I can't think further than trying to reach out to Natalya somehow, trying to make the school change its mind about the showcase, about her role in it, about waiting.

The casting is going to be posted at six p.m. in the main hallway—right after history class.

Nick's waiting for me outside the classroom. "People are fucking crazy," he says as he takes my hand in his. He takes my hand in front of everyone, not caring who sees us, not caring if someone could tell his parents, my parents, my brother. I stare at our hands together. It feels so right. Last summer, when we decided to become friends with certain benefits for a limited time, he never held my hand like this when there were a lot of people we knew around. Sometimes the secret was thrilling but more times than not, it was oppressing.

He leans in to me. "Are you nervous?"

"I feel like I want to throw up and I'm not sure if it's the results, knowing Nata won't be first like she should be, or knowing I have to talk to my dad as soon as possible."

"Did you talk to Rob?"

"Not yet. He's super busy preparing for a prize application. His professor wants him to apply to this Greenberg prize for young physicists."

Kayode taps Nick on the shoulder. "Wow, wow, wow, isn't that Nick Grawski holding the hand of a girl?"

"I know you wish I was holding yours," Nick jokes but Kayode's voice was so loud some people turn to us, including Jen. She stares at our joined hands but doesn't say a word and slides past a small group of students to make her way to the board.

More and more people stare at us.

I don't want to feel hopeful.

I don't want to feel full of dreams.

I don't want to feel like maybe, just maybe Nick's right, and I will get the role. It would be over Nata's accident—would it even be fair?

But a small part of me still clings to the idea that it could be mine, that Nick and I could both hold the leads of the showcase, that everyone would be so proud of me, that for once I know where I belong.

And then, Jen screams, "Yes!" with her fist up in the air.

My hopes crumble at my feet and my stomach is in knots.

I'm not good enough. Simply not good enough.

There are whispers around us. Nick's hand tightens around mine. My eyes glaze over the list and I'm happy to see his name right by the role of Prince Charming.

My name's not anywhere to be seen.

At least not at the top.

It's toward the bottom. I didn't even get one of the main parts. I worked so hard. I don't understand.

But then Nick points to the top again.

Understudy of Sleeping Beauty—Emilia Moretti.

I'm going to be learning right alongside Jen.

CHAPTER 22 - NICK

SHE'S STANDING THERE, completely frozen. And she's not smiling. She turns to me and whispers, "And now what?"

"Now, we—you and I are going to fucking show the world how amazing and talented you are."

Her finger points at the line with her name. "It doesn't make sense," she says. "Why would I be Jen's understudy?"

Emilia tenses. I'm sure that's not her ideal scenario, but that means the School trusts her enough, trusts her skills enough to have her become the lead in the showcase if something ever happens to Jen. Being an understudy when you're a junior like she is clearly means they're preparing her for a big role next year.

Her shoulders slouch for a split second, but then she straightens up. "Nonna's going to be so disappointed. And my parents. They spend thousands of dollars on my education, on me being here, and that's how I repay them." She sighs and with all the

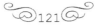

people surrounding us, it's not the moment to tell her that her parents aren't paying the School a dime these days. "I'm happy for you," she continues and her smile isn't forced. She takes my hand in hers and everything feels more real: her, me, us, the part. "You're going to be amazing." I guide her away from the crowd.

"What's wrong?" I ask.

And she huffs. "Nothing."

"When you're pursing your lips like this, something is wrong. You only do that when you're holding something back. Don't hold back."

"It's…I mean I'd understand if you don't have time for, you know…" she stutters. And then sighs loudly. "Us. If you decide you don't have time for us."

"This is a joke, right?"

"Not a funny one."

"I don't care if you're first or last in the showcase. You're talented but you're much more than that." I run my finger on her cheek. "I care about the way you put other people first, I care about the way you always find something to smile about, I care about the way you make me feel."

"And how is that?"

"Like I'm the king of the world."

She cracks a smile and I do feel like the king of the world. "I can't believe you're referencing *Titanic*. You said that movie was the stupidest ever made, that they could have both fit on that raft."

I wink at her. "Being the understudy is not a bad thing," I say more seriously, and my hand goes up and down her arm. She leans into me. "Being the understudy means they believe in you, that they want you to be the one next year."

"I know you're right, but I had this fairy tale in my mind of how everything was going to go, how I was going to make it to the top and finally make everyone proud."

"You need to make yourself proud," I reply.

She raises an eyebrow. "You should listen to yourself from time to time—you don't give too shitty advice."

"Trust me, I'm trying."

She nudges me. "Congrats on getting the top spot. I knew you would." She glances at the floor and then right at me. There's so much in her eyes, questions and desire. "So...you and me?"

I lean in and kiss her. It's not the kiss I wish to give her, but it's already something. There are some people whooping in the background, but I don't care and she doesn't seem to either—she smiles against my lips. "You love to answer questions with demonstrations, and I kind of love that." She bites her lip. "I still can't believe Nata's not on the list. I still can't believe she's not going to make it to the showcase. I tried calling her mom but didn't get any answers. I don't have her uncle's number and I don't know how to get any news from her."

"We'll ask Svetlana, I'm sure she knows something."

But Svetlana doesn't know anything. No one knows anything. Rumors spread that Natalya's father was depressed, that maybe it wasn't an accident after all.

And Em defends Natalya, she reminds everyone how much Natalya wanted this and that no one should be speaking the way they are, like they know anything.

And then she leaves yet another voice mail that stays unanswered.

CHAPTER 23 - EM

I CAN'T BELIEVE IT.

I can't believe I got understudy. It's not the role I wanted, and it's not the role that will make everyone see me differently, but it's such a big deal. I know it is. I'm only a junior—the chance for me to get that spot was so rare. I should feel happy, I should feel elated, I should feel something more than my hands getting clammy and my throat tightening with anxiety.

I haven't even called my parents yet. I should. I need to tell Nonna. I need to tell all of them.

I glance around the room; Nata's stuff is everywhere. Her pictures and her clothes, and the motivational cards she stuck on her dresser.

Like this one from Misty Copeland. I just try to approach every *opportunity* on stage, as if it's my first time and my last time. Nata does that, she really does.

The pictures of her mom when she danced in San Francisco.

The pictures of her friend, Becca. The one she used to call so often but not anymore.

She'd be first. She'd feel something. She'd be ecstatic.

Nick called his mom to let him know, and I could hear her squeal through the phone. His mom never squeals.

I can do this.

I have to do this.

I pick up my phone and dial Nonna's phone number first. "Bellisima!"

I take a deep breath. "Hi! I got the audition results."

"If you didn't get it, then it's not meant to be. And they're idiots. Don't sound sad."

"No, I'm disappointed, that's all. I didn't get it!"

"Oh Bellisima, it's okay. I know you really wanted it. You worked so hard for it." She sounds more tired than the last time we talked.

"I didn't get the main part, but I'm the understudy for the main role. I'm going to learn so much," I reply and cringe thinking I'm going to have to learn with Jen. I'm going to have to see Jen dance with Nick every single day.

"Congratulations, Bellisima. So proud of you." She coughs. And coughs. And coughs.

"Nonna!" Panic rises through me. Why is she coughing so much? What's going on?

She wheezes. "I'm fine. Fine."

I don't believe her. "I could come over tonight."

"Don't be silly, Bellisima. You need to stay and rest—I'm sure you've got lots of training planned in the next days."

"You need to rest too. I'll try to come over before the weekend."

"I love you, Bellisima. With or without that role, you understand me?"

It's almost like she hugs me via the phone with those words. Like she knows exactly what I need to hear. "I love you too, Nonna."

I hang up and stare at the phone. I need to call my parents, so one of them checks on Nonna. But I won't be able to keep my mouth shut about Claire Carter. I won't.

I dial Mom's number. She picks up on the first ring. "So? How did you do?" There's so much hope in her voice, and I remember why I needed to be first in the first place.

"I didn't get it."

"Oh." She pauses. "You still have next year, right?"

"Yes. I still have next year." I inhale and exhale, trying to find a happy place within me. "I did get the understudy."

"That's good, right? I mean they must see something in you, honey, if they gave you that position."

I know she doesn't mean to be hurtful. My mom never wants to hurt anyone, she's one of the sweetest people I know, but her words still cut through me. I remember how when I was about eight, she told me about how she always wanted to be a ballerina, how she thought I was going to love dancing, how I

really needed to give it my best. And then I think about Claire. Claire who wrapped me into that ballerina blanket, and that ballerina onesie. And then about Dad, who told me so many times that I really need to get my act together because their money is running out and my school is so expensive that I wonder what he's going to say.

"Honey? It's good. You did good." She sounds reassuring now, apologetic even.

"It is definitely a step up."

"How did Natalya do?"

I tell her what happened to Nata and then about Nick getting the main part. She's so excited for him, telling me that's going to be me next year, and I don't have the heart to tell her that I'm not sure dancing even makes me happy anymore.

"You need to tell your dad about your understudy part. He's going to be so proud of you."

"If he doesn't have time…that's okay."

"No time for his one and only daughter?" She laughs. "I don't think so. He's watching TV. He's going to be so proud. Let me call him."

"Okay. And Mom?"

"What sweetie?"

"do you think you could check on Nonna? She doesn't sound good."

"Of course, I will. Dino?" she calls my dad. My dad who used to be my hero, but who ever since he got fired and got this new job, is more and more bitter and less willing to forgive and forget.

"Hi," he says. And his voice is hard. "I know what you're going to tell me."

"What?"

"I know what you're going to tell me and I don't want to talk about it."

I'm confused. "How do you know? Did Mom already tell you?"

"Your boyfriend's father called me to let me know he blabbered to his useless son."

"What?" I can't believe he's talking like this. I can't believe he's so mad. I can't believe he's the same man who only a few months ago sang Christmas carols at the dinner table with all of us.

"I don't want you seeing Nicholas."

"And I want to know what my story is, I want to know why you're talking to me like this. You told me they tried to sell me. Is everything you ever told me a lie? When you told me I meant as much to you as Roberto does, was it also a lie?" I take a deep breath. This outburst has taken a lot out of me.

"I don't understand why you want to know so much. Don't we love you? Aren't we enough for you?"

"Dino, what's going on?" I hear Mom in the background and if there's one person I don't want to hurt, it's her. She's been so supportive through everything that has been going on. Nonna's the glue that holds us all together but Mom's the rock that keeps us stable. She's the one who can get through to Dad.

"Nothing, honey."

"Your mom's not picking up her phone, I'll go and check on her. Tell Em again how proud I am of her."

There's a shuffle and Dad's on the line. "I'm guessing congrats are in order." His voice is much lower. He sounds like himself again, like maybe my success makes up for my questions.

"Dad, I need to know."

He sighs. "No, you don't need to know. You need to leave this alone. Please."

"Is Claire really my mother? Did you maybe, I don't know, get me illegally? I'd understand if you did. I'd understand, I promise."

"I'm going to hang up, Emilia. I don't want to talk to you when you're like this. And let me tell you something else: I don't want you hanging out with Nick any longer. His father is not a good influence and apples don't fall far from the tree."

"And I want to know what happened. I want to know!"

"I want you to drop it. Drop the topic. And I don't want to hear from Roberto or anyone else that you're with Nick."

"Or what? What are you going to do, Dad? You've got nothing! You don't want to tell me what's going on, you don't want to tell me the truth. You don't want to stand up for whatever it is you did!"

He hangs up before I can continue ranting.

So when my phone rings again thirty minutes later and I see it's home calling me, my stomach tightens and my tone is curt. "I'm not going to stop seeing Nick!" I say.

"Oh Emilia, sweetie." Mom's voice cuts through my heart. She's crying and her voice is made of tears. "Oh honey. I'm sorry. I'm so sorry."

ALWAYS SECOND BEST

"What's going on?" The words are barely above a whisper and my entire body shakes. I know from her voice. I know in my heart what she's about to tell me, but I don't want to believe it. I don't want to hear it.

I close my eyes.

"It's Nonna, sweetie. She's…she's gone."

And I bury my head in my knees, dropping the phone on the floor. I think I let out a muffled scream. I think tears fall down my face. I think my heart loses a piece that I'll never find again.

Everything stops. Everything's a blur. Everything should stop if it hasn't. My heart fills with nothing else but sadness and regret.

I pick up the phone again, bring it to my ear. "Honey?" Mom calls and I realize I haven't talked in a few minutes.

"Mmm-hmm." I don't trust my vocal cords. At all.

"You need to come home, baby."

"She's really dead, isn't she?" The feeling of dread is overwhelming.

"Yes, baby. She's gone." And Mom sounds like she did the first time I fell from my bike, the first time kids made fun of me because I was adopted, the first time I saw Nick kissing someone else.

But I didn't know sadness before, I didn't know what it's like to realize I'm never going to see her again, I'm never going to enter the restaurant and hear her voice. I'm never going to call her again and listen to her laugh.

"Do you want me to come and pick you up?"

"No. No. I'll come later. I need…I need some time." Even though I want to be with Mom and Dad right now, I also simply want to stay here and cry and not move. And I know Mom would be worried about me breaking down like this, and I want to be able to be there for her too.

"Does Roberto know?"

"Your dad called him."

"Okay. Mom?"

"What, honey?"

Tears muffle my voice. "Nonna told me…" I blabber and take a second to compose myself. "She told me how amazing you are. She says…" Another deep breath. "She said that we're all lucky to have you."

Mom sniffles. "Thank you." She pauses. "I love you, honey. Come home whenever you can."

We hang up and I lie on my bed. Sobs rack through my body. And I have a hard time breathing. She can't be gone. She can't be gone. She can't be gone.

I don't know how much time passes. I need to get up and go home.

It's dark in my room and outside when there's a knock at my door. Roberto enters and I struggle to come down the bunk bed ladder.

Roberto crosses the room in two strides instead of the four it would normally take and shakes his head, crying as he opens his arms. I rush to him and lean into his embrace. "I was supposed to call her," he says. "I was supposed to call her yesterday and I didn't. I got so wrapped up in an experiment that by the time I was done, it was too late."

"She knows…" I catch myself. "She knew how much your studies mean to you. She knew it."

"But not more than her. They didn't mean more than her."

I hold him until he stops crying, until he has no tears left, and then I call Mom to let her know we're going to leave the School soon. She says not to hurry, that they're deep in paperwork and calling the family, that knowing Roberto and I are together right now is making it easier for her to concentrate on what needs to get done. "How is Dad?" I ask.

"He stayed with her as long as possible," she replies. "And he's muttering. I think he's talking to her. A mixture of Italian and English. I've never seen him like this." She pauses. "You kids take your time. I love you both."

"We love you too, Mommy." I haven't called her mommy in such a long time.

Roberto and I lie side by side on the floor. "When I told her I was gay, she told me to be with someone who makes me smile and happy and gives me flutters. And then she said, if he has to have a you-know-what to make that happen, then so be it. Be happy." Roberto chuckles. "And when she met Giovanni, she took me aside and told me to treat him well, because I didn't want to let go of someone who made me smile so widely and without restraint." He pauses. "She also told me to get off your back when it comes to Nick."

"She knew what she was talking about." I push myself back up and sit down. "It's like it's not true, like I'm going to call her and she's going to say it was all a stupid mistake of this modern medicine, as she liked to call it. That she's well and fine."

"I remember after her stroke, she wanted me to promise to her that we'd be sad but happy whenever she passed away. That we needed to be happy for her, because she believed in something bigger. She believed she'd be seeing Poppa again and all the ones that went too young, too soon."

I sniffle and wipe my snot with my arm. "Dad must be so devastated," I say. "We got into this big fight today, and while we were fighting Nonna was dying."

"I got into a fight with Dad too…yesterday. We can't see eye to eye on anything. I don't know what's going on with him. I don't know…he hadn't seen Nonna in an entire week, and he lives right next door to her. Mom does everything. She takes care of everything."

"Nick's dad told him there was more to my adoption than what we found out last summer."

Roberto sighs. "I'm sorry. I'm sorry about everything. I know we haven't talked about it for a very long time, but I know I fucked up."

"When?"

"When you started looking for your family… sometimes, it almost feels like you think we're not enough. Or at least I thought so, until I realized how difficult it must be for you."

"What?"

Roberto levels his eyes with me. "To try to fit everyone's expectations of you."

ALWAYS SECOND BEST

I clear my throat and glance away. "It's not really trying to fit the expectations as much as trying to make people proud. I don't know, it's like I haven't found my place yet."

"And Nick?"

"What about him?"

"Are you guys…you know…back together?"

"Do you really want to know?"

"Yes."

"Then, yes. We are. Dad doesn't want us to be together and with Nonna and everything, I don't know."

Roberto tilts my chin toward him and bores his dark eyes into mine. His tone is the most serious I've ever heard. "You know I'm older than you, right?"

"Not much older. And definitely not much wiser."

"Nonna was right about us needing to be with people who make us laugh, who make us feel, and when she said to make sure we stay in the moment. Nick's good for you. He's good for you now, and maybe still next year or in two years. Don't let Dad stay in the way of that. Don't let his dad stay in the way of that. And…" He pauses. "Don't let me stay in the way of that either."

My emotions are all over the place; they jump from gratitude to sadness, from happiness to devastation in seconds.

"I didn't get the main role in the showcase."

"Who the fuck cares? I don't even think you want it."

"Of course I do."

He shakes his head. "Fine, I'll keep my wisdom on that particular topic for another day." He wraps his arm around my shoulder. "Let's go home."

CHAPTER 24 - NICK

EM'S NOT AT school the next day. Of course, everyone already knows about her grandmother, but some are arguing she's never coming back because she lost it after becoming Jen's understudy.

I swear I would have thought dancing for so many hours a day would leave them too exhausted to start up stories.

Right after my math class, I head to the first official rehearsal. The showcase is in three months and while we've all been rehearsing bits and pieces of it for the past seven months, it's still the first time I enter the room as Prince Charming.

And I can't deny that feels pretty good.

Jen strides my way as soon as she sees me. She's smiling and her dark eyes are done over the top today, but as always, she's gorgeous. Her mom's black and her dad's Asian and she's got legs that don't end and yes, I was attracted to her the very first time we went out. But we don't really talk, and the chemistry kind of fizzled out pretty fast too.

"Hey." She nudges me. "I knew we would make it."

"Congrats," I reply.

Her smile dims. "I know if Nata hadn't gotten into this car accident, I wouldn't be standing here. They might have put me as her understudy, which would have been so humiliating."

I raise an eyebrow.

She blabbers. "Because I'm a senior. Not a freaking junior like Emilia." She glances around. "I can't believe she's missing the first big rehearsal."

"Why can't you believe it? Her grandmother passed away, what did you want her to do?" I sound harsh but I can't help it.

"I didn't know."

"You're the only one in this school," I mutter.

"I swear I didn't know. I turned off all social media until the big day—I don't want to read how much I suck until then."

I raise an eyebrow.

"I'm sorry about Em's grandmother." She actually does look sorry. But then she touches my arm. "Are you two…you know, serious?"

"Yes," I reply. "We are. This time, we really are." And I try to make sure she understands the meaning behind my words.

She flinches but then her smile's back on. "We'll see. You are going to spend a lot of time with me."

I sigh. "What I meant to say is you and I are not getting back together. You're a nice girl, but…"

ALWAYS SECOND BEST

"I know—I'm a nice girl, but I'm simply not it. I've heard that before." She turns around. "Anyways, we've got a lot to do." She sounds robotic, as if my words had actually hurt her. I've never thought she wanted anything else. She's never mentioned anything, never complained about me not being really present when we were together.

I thought she was fine with it, that we were kind of using one another, but I guess not. And I feel like a jerk.

I hurry to her. "Jen, you know that…"

She waves her hand in the air. "I don't want to hear it. It's going to be sad and pathetic and it's going to make you look bad and me look way too needy for my own taste. Whatever, I got it." She turns around. "But honestly, you and Em better get your shit together. Because one." She raises a finger up. "You have no idea how lucky you are to be together and all that jazz, and two." She raises another one. "This showcase is my way to the top, it's my way to show everyone that I earned it. That it's mine. And I can't do that if you're not doing your best."

She stares at me, her dark eyes almost trying to probe my very soul. "I won't fuck it up. I won't fuck up anything."

Her lips turn slightly upward; it's not a full smile, but it's there. "I wouldn't go that far. I only asked you to do two things correctly—the rest is up to you."

She hurries to the center of the room. Svetlana's waiting for us.

And the show must go on.

CHAPTER 25 - EM

THE CHURCH IS COLD. Of course it is—the weather's gotten slightly better, but the temperature's still hesitating between freezing and letting us believe spring might be around the corner.

The church is cold and Nana hated being cold. She loved watching snow falling down and seeing the entire neighborhood turn into a snowy fairy tale, as she'd like to call it, but if she was inside her house, she wanted to be warm.

The church is cold and the tension in my family adds a certain bite to it.

Roberto wraps his arm around my shoulder. The church is full and Dad and Mom are talking to the priest for one last-minute check. Mom is doing most of the talking. Dad's been in his own world ever since Nonna passed. Mom is bringing him food when he doesn't want to sit with us at dinner, she's the one who took care of most of the paperwork, she's organizing

everything. It almost seems like he's not realizing what's happening.

"All our condolences." A lady who's wearing a Chanel suit similar to the one Mom gave away in an auction last year squeezes my shoulder. "Your grandmother was the kindest and most spirited soul I've ever met." She smiles and her gray eyes assess me. "She said you were like her. She loved you both so very much." She continues glancing between me and Roberto.

"Thank you," we both whisper and she turns around, sitting all the way in the back. The church is packed. Nonna's restaurant was the place to be in the neighborhood and everyone seems to want to pay their respects.

Mr. Edwards is sitting on the other side of me. And his silent tears are worse than all the sobbing in the world. He's whispering something, and I'm not sure if it's a prayer or a message to her.

Roberto shivers and I turn back to him. "Are you okay? You look super pale."

He coughs. "I'm fine. My stomach has been bothering me and I just got a cold." He pauses. "Is Nick here?"

I don't need to turn around and look in the crowd to know the answer. "He is. How about you? Have you heard from Giovanni?"

"He wanted to come, but it's way too expensive to fly right now and he's saving money." He takes a deep breath and winces. "He did order flowers, orchids." He tilts his chin toward Dad. "I'm sorry about Dad being a jerk."

"Don't worry about it. Dad has a lot more to deal with right now, anyways."

"When did you turn so wise?" he asks and coughs again; this time it sounds more like a wheeze.

"Maybe you should go see a doctor."

"You sound like Giovanni."

"I knew I liked him for a reason." I nudge him. "But no kiddin', you don't sound good."

He sighs. "I'll be fine. I should know, right?"

I may have rolled my eyes at him before, but not today. Today, I lean into his shoulder. "Take care of yourself."

"Promise."

Mom and Dad shake the priest's hand and go back to their seats. Mom's on my side, while Dad's on Roberto's side. Mom's shoulders tremble slightly, as if she's trying to keep all the sadness inside of her but it's pouring out nonetheless, while Dad doesn't say a word, he just stares straight ahead.

When the coffin enters the church, carried by the gentlemen of the funeral home, the weight on my chest deepens, threatening to split it open. I can't believe Nonna's in there, that I will never see her again. I inhale deeply and Mom's hand finds mine and I take Roberto's in mine. Nonna said the biggest strength came from family, that we should never forget that family comes first.

After the church, where I had to convince myself this was really happening, that this wasn't a nightmare…

ALWAYS SECOND BEST

After the cemetery, where seeing the tombstone lowered into the ground sent a new wave of sadness coursing through me, where I tried to hold myself straight and tall, where I tried to be strong for my parents and Roberto...

After the gathering at the restaurant, where people brought food, comfort, soothing words, tears, funny and sad memories...

I hide away.

I'm hiding in the small walkway past Nonna's bedroom. That's the place I stomped to one day after my parents had told me I couldn't buy an expensive doll at the store. They'd said that we didn't get to buy everything just because we had money. Nonna had found me here and she'd caressed my head. She whispered, "If you want that doll very badly, I'll get it for you." But I told her no—I couldn't bring myself to go against my parents, and deep inside, I'd realized she wasn't as well off as we were. When I shook my head, she hugged me without a word and then smiled. "We could make our own doll. Go apologize to your parents, and then I'll show you how to make clothes for the dolls you already have."

I sniffle.

I should go back to the crowd, to my parents, to Roberto, to all our friends. But I'm too sad. Too sad to continue mingling. Too sad to pretend that I'm fine. Too sad.

There are footsteps in the hallway and I almost expect to see Nonna poking her head in and laughing at finding me here again.

But the tall frame isn't Nonna's. Nick's standing in front of me, wearing a dark suit that hugs his shoulders, but he's pulling on his shirt. He told me once he feels like he can't breathe when he wears a tie.

"Hey," Nick says and his voice is low, careful. It's the same voice he used once when we tried to rescue a stray cat. He's not crowding me, like he knows I need to be the one to initiate any contact right now.

"Hey," I reply.

"Your Nonna told me to continue fighting for you."

I raise one eyebrow, leaning against the wall to face him. "When did she say that?"

"At Christmas," he replies. "I was trying so hard to tell you how sorry I was, to tell you how much you mean to me, but you kept me at a distance, and then you said you were seeing someone, and your Nonna came to me after dessert, she sat next to me on the couch and she put her hand on my thigh. She leaned in and she said, 'Nicholas.'" He pauses and I smile slightly. She loved calling him Nicholas or Nicos. "'Nicos,' she said, 'I know you can do well by my granddaughter. I know you made mistakes and I know you regret them. You need to tell her, you need to give her the space she needs, but you need to make sure you're there for her. She'll open her eyes.' And then she kissed my cheek and she continued by saying, 'You're a good boy. Make sure you become an even better man one day.'"

"That sounds like her." I sigh. "But clearly you didn't listen to her—you went to that New Year's Eve party and you almost kissed Nata." I hate my voice for breaking but it's too much. Everything's too much. All the emotions. Everything I've kept bottled inside, it's too much: not getting the main part, the past, losing Nonna. "You pushed me away. And Nonna...Nonna didn't know everything. Maybe if she did, she wouldn't have rooted for us the way she did. Maybe, she would have told me to move on and would have told you the same."

"Do you really think so?" His tone's still soothing, but my blood's boiling and everything within me is confused and angry and desperate. "At that New Year's party, I had told myself this would be the day I'd finally come clean about everything. That it would be the day I'd admit how much I've missed you. But when I got there, I heard you were there with a guy."

"I wasn't!"

"I didn't know. You told me you were starting to date someone who meant a lot to you."

"I never did. I haven't dated anyone since last summer, while you clearly had no issues dating yourself. You went out with Jen and Sandra and whoever else." My voice rises. Nonna's not there to tell me it's all going to be fine.

"I didn't want to go out with them." He rubs the back of his neck and this time his voice hitches. He walks a bit closer to me. "It was my dad. I had to go out with them for my dad."

"Bullshit."

"I wish it was bullshit—I'd be an asshole, but at least my father wouldn't be using me. It'd be my decision and not his. You have no idea how much worse it is when you're forced to be an asshole."

My head pounds and my heart skips a beat. "I don't get it."

He doesn't glance away from me and I can see him wince. "For the past two years or so, Daddy Dearest has asked me to help him with business stuff: ranging from picking documents up for him, participating in charity balls and those stupid auctions, to dating daughters of business partners."

"That doesn't make sense."

"I'm starting to think it was more a way to keep me away from you than to really help his business deals."

"But why did you do it? Why? Why after this summer?"

"I promised to take Jen out after this summer in exchange for Claire Carter's mailing address."

"Oh."

"I didn't want to. I swear I didn't want to. But the more I think about it and the more I look at all the times he tried to get me to go out with one of his business partners' daughters, the more I realize it was right around the times we got closer together. Remember the winter holidays two years ago?"

I nod. That winter, Nick and I spent every afternoon together. At his place or my place. Roberto was sometimes with us, but mostly he was reading scientific paper after scientific paper, trying to find the best project for a physics fair. Nick's father walked in on us in his bedroom. We weren't doing anything... I was hoping he would hold my hand, we were watching *Titanic* on TV. And he was making fun of it. And my entire body was already in tune with his. I imagined our first kiss, I imagined how it would feel to have my hand in his. I imagined how it would be to walk side by side with him.

"Do you remember how my dad freaked out on us?"

I nod again. His dad opened the door and told him we needed to watch TV downstairs and that we weren't allowed in the same room by ourselves.

"Three days after that, he asked me to go out with Sina. I was fifteen and was going through my I-don't-think-so stage. He told me if I didn't, he would stop paying my tuition. So I did." He pauses. "Plus I was fifteen. I thought going out with Sina wasn't too bad."

I flinch and he must see it because his words stumble out of his mouth, uncoordinated. "What I mean is that I was fifteen, and I thought my father was being his usual ass self. But it only happened whenever he saw us getting closer. Whenever I mentioned something I liked about you..." He pauses.

I step closer to him. "Why didn't you tell me before? We told each other everything."

"Because I didn't want to appear less in your eyes. What guy can't even stand up to his own father?"

"Standing up to your own parents is usually the easiest part and the hardest part about being our age." My voice trembles at the memory of my grandmother telling me this one evening after making me some tea. "Nonna said that to me."

"She was amazing," Nick says and I gently take his hand in mine, bring it to my face. He cups it and I lean into it. "She loved you so much." He kisses my forehead, my eyes, my nose. "I...I love you," he whispers and I inhale sharply. My fingers shake as I bring my hand to his arm. "I love you," he repeats.

And he kisses me. Tender and passionate. Desperate and hopeful.

I forget myself into his lips. Into the way he tastes, the way my entire body reacts to his, the way his arms tighten around my waist.

"What do you think you're doing?" my father's voice booms.

CHAPTER 26 - NICK

EM JUMPS AWAY. She's not hiding but she's not standing tall. And she glances from her father to me.

And I stand there, not wanting to make a scene, but my annoyance ripples through me like the ricochet we used to try to do on the sea at the Hamptons. They sunk pretty easily, and now my angers sinks into my veins right along with them.

"What do you think you're doing?" he asks again.

"I'm sorry if that was inappropriate, sir, or not the right time. But I'm not sorry I kissed your daughter, sir." I've never called him sir before, but it seems fitting.

"I told you, Emilia. I told you I didn't want you seeing him."

Emilia takes my hand in hers, stepping closer to me. "And I told you I don't care."

"This is not the time nor the place to talk about this. This is not the time nor the place to make a scene."

"No one is making a scene but you." Em tries to sound strong, but her voice isn't as sure as before, and I for sure don't want to turn Nonna's funeral into a let's-make-a-scene day. I may disagree with most of my father's educational lessons, but his reinforcing that there's a time to be quiet might not be all wrong.

Plus I'm still unsure of what went down in their business. It seems like shutting up might be the best solution now, but I also don't want to let Emilia bear all her father's wrath.

Dino points his finger at me. "You need to stay away from my daughter. She doesn't need someone like you in her life. Someone who does everything his dad asks even if it breaks her heart." His voice rises with each word. "And she doesn't need someone whose father breaks the law like it's nothing. Who lets go of his friend and business partner when the going gets rough. You know what they say: the apple doesn't fall far from the tree."

I kiss Em on the cheek and whisper, "I'll call you later." She doesn't let go of my hand but instead stands right in front of me, as if to shield me even though I'm much bigger than her and am almost a head taller than her father. "I can't believe you're talking to him like this. I can't believe you're doing this. Now."

"I can't believe you're doing this now of all days!" he shouts, and my eyes dart to the stairs. People must hear him.

"Come on, let's go," I tell Em and try to pull her with me, but she's having none of it.

"You've fallen far. You said apples don't fall far from the tree? What would Nonna say about you right now? Nonna would never have treated anyone the way you're treating Nick. She would never…" She inhales deeply and blinks rapidly. She's clearly trying to prevent the tears from falling. She's clearly trying to hold her own. She's clearly trying to find the place within herself that gives her some peace, some sense of justice.

Dino opens his mouth and closes it. And then sobs crack his entire body. He's holding on to Em, who opens her arms to him, to comfort him.

Because despite everything, she can't push him away. Despite everything, he's her father. And they're both suffering.

She gives me a look and a small smile and I nod and I let them grieve.

CHAPTER 27 - EM

I'M FURIOUS WITH HIM, livid. But we're both so broken over the loss of Nonna that we cling to one another, unable to support ourselves individually. And so I squeeze him and I shower his embrace with my tears, letting him do the same. I don't know what this means. Is it a breakthrough between us? Will things go back to the way they were?

But when he pulls away, he won't look at me. And that's fine because my anger's still simmering in my veins. And we don't speak again for the rest of the day. Not the rest of the weekend, either. Mom continues to try so hard, but it's like he's not there. And I'm sure she sees through the fake half smiles, the fake conversations, the faking touching of their hands at the dinner table.

I'm not hungry. Sadness settles in my chest and my stomach. Nonna's never going to sit with us again and my Sunday nights won't be spent with her. I clear my throat—even though the entire table fell silent about five minutes ago. "I need to leave before five, need to make it back on time. I have to catch up."

Roberto coughs several times and holds himself on the chair. "I need to go back to the university too. I need to use that dorm they're giving me for free, otherwise they might take it away from me."

"You need to stay here and rest," Mom tells him. "You're sounding worse and worse by the second."

"My back's hurting a bit, I'm telling you it's a bad cold." He stands up and quickly touches the top of my head. "I'll call you tonight," he tells me, and I'm not sure if he needs to talk or if he knows I'm going to need to talk. I need to ask him what he thinks I should do about Dad, if I should tell Mom.

"Do you want me to ride the train with you?"

"Are you kidding? That'd take you forever. Don't worry about it." He grabs his shoulder bag by the entrance. Mom gets up and goes with him. Dad doesn't even say a word. Not a goodbye, not have a good week, not a feel better.

He stares into his plate and then stands up and gets out of the kitchen.

When Mom gets back, I help her put the plates and the dinner away in silence. We had leftovers from what people brought us and every bite was difficult to swallow. I'm sure we all thought about Nonna. Last week I was with her, eating and laughing and asking her advice about Nick. Once we're done, Mom washes her hand and sighs. "Your dad will come around. It's hard on him right now."

"I know it's hard on him. But Mom..." I glance at her and she looks so tired, so worn out, so sad. "Never mind."

She kisses my cheek. "I know it's hard on you too and I know how much you loved Nonna and how everything must seem too much. When it comes to Nick, you also need to give your Dad some time."

"I don't understand him. I'm seventeen. Next year, I'll be eighteen. I'm responsible, I'm here, I try my hardest."

"Yes, you do. But you're seventeen..."

"I am. I am seventeen. Next year I'll be turning eighteen and I'll be allowed to vote. But Dad still thinks I can't decide who to date?"

"When I turned eighteen, my mom told me that turning eighteen wasn't suddenly going to make her and my dad stop being my parents. I never thought I'd have to tell you this." She sounds tired and I'm tempted to stop talking—I don't want to argue with her. She pulls me into a hug. "I'll talk to your father."

"Mom?"

"What, honey?"

"I love you," I tell her because that's all I can say right now. Asking her about Dad doesn't feel right. Trying to justify myself, to explain why I think Dad's wrong, doesn't feel right.

"I love you too," she answers but even as I glance up at her and she smiles, I see that she's full of sadness.

At school, I avoid people and head straight to my dorm. Don't feel like doing small talk right now. I want to talk to Roberto, maybe call Nick too, and then sleep. Or try to sleep. I haven't heard anything about Natalya's condition, Natalya ever since her accident, despite calling her mom several times.

I hurry down the hallway and storm into my room, dropping my bag onto its usual spot—except there's already a bag there.

What the heck?

I turn around and Jen's sitting on what used to be Natalya's bed. Her dark black hair is a bit messy— very unusual for her. She's wearing sweatpants and a large shirt that says "I love Paris." And I think I spot one pimple on her cheek. The world is about to fall. She's not smiling but she's not scowling either. It's the most neutral I've seen her.

"What are you doing here?" At least I don't sound mean, only surprised.

"I don't want to be here either, but apparently it'd be good for us to share a room, since you're my understudy and all." She emphasizes the word "understudy," but I don't even think she's doing it on purpose. It must be automatic.

"That doesn't make any sense."

"Tell me about it." She sighs and stands up. "One, I get to room with a junior, two, that junior is you, and three, I really don't want to sleep in Natalya's bed."

"Where's all of her stuff?" Everything's gone: the poster of the ballerina flying in the air, her Tolstoy books that she got from her grandmother, her pictures.

It's like she's never even been in this school. It's like she's never been my roommate. It's like whatever she didn't achieve means more than what she did achieve.

"I didn't touch them, if that's what you're saying." Jen sounds like she's struggling not to get mad. Welcome to the club.

"That's not what I said."

"Her uncle came to pick up everything," she replies.

"Is she awake? Is she okay? Did he say anything?" My mind races. I haven't heard anything about her, and her uncle left me only one voice mail to tell me he would update me, but there was no news

"She's awake."

The pressure on my chest lightens.

"She's been awake." She pauses. "Her uncle was sorry he didn't let us know earlier. Apparently she wants to go back on stage as soon as possible, but her uncle said she's going to need physical rehabilitation for several months. He sounded so sad and he gave me Natalya's mother's new number." She nibbles on her thumb—one of the only signs that she's either worried or sad. Jen usually doesn't show her feelings. "He said we should contact her to get in touch with Natalya." Her voice lowers and I'm not sure if she's talking to me or herself. "I can't imagine how hard it's going to be for her."

"We should try to do something."

"I honestly don't know what would make her feel better—except dancing again." Jen nibbles on the skin of her index finger before putting it behind her back. "I'm sorry about your grandmother."

I glance around. "My Nonna would tell me that us rooming together would be the perfect opportunity to realize we're not so different from one another after all."

"Your Nonna would have been wrong on that one." Jen bites her lip. "I really am sorry, I've heard how close you were to her."

And she sounds sincere—there's no snark, not a tinge of irony into her words. "Thank you."

She shrugs and waves her hand in the air. "We're going to need rules. Nick cannot come hang out here all the time. One, it would be weird because you know I kissed him too. Like our lips touched the same guys' lips. It's almost like we kissed."

"I've never realized you talk a lot."

"I've never needed to talk to you." She pauses. "Anyways, that was the number one rule. The second one is don't crowd me, I don't need hours-long conversations into the night and I don't need friends."

"You don't?"

"Friends skew feelings. I don't want to start liking you and feeling sorry for you—it might throw me off my game."

"You got the part, you do realize that, right?"

"See…that puppy face of yours is already starting to get to me. I know I've got the part, and I deserve the part. You take dancing for granted. I never will." She turns to her desk as if the conversation was over, but then she sighs. "Third rule, if you're really feeling down, you can talk to me. I'm not sure I'll answer, but you can talk to me."

I raise an eyebrow and she turns back to me right at this moment. "Okay, that's creepy. You and Nick already have the same ticks."

This brings a smile to my face and she shrugs only one shoulder. "I put a picture of you and Nata on your bed. Her uncle said you could have it." She grabs some clothes in the closet. "And that's already way too much talking. I'm going to take a shower and once I'm back, we can get back to ignoring one another. At least for a little while."

"Sounds like a plan," I reply and even though this was one of the weirdest conversations ever, it also showed me a different side of Jen.

Maybe Nonna would have been right after all.

Maybe Jen and I could be friends.

CHAPTER 28 - NICK

"EMILIA: DO IT AGAIN!" Svetlana calls out. Em's breathing hard, but she raises her arms above her head. "More grace, Emilia. You have to feel the movement through your fingertips." Em lowers her arms and then brings them up again. She's concentrating too hard.

"No!" Svetlana snaps. "Emilia, try it from the very beginning."

Em purses her lips, but doesn't protest and gets in position again.

Jen clears her throat. "I know you've got your love story going on, but we're supposed to rehearse too. Eduardo said our second act was, and I quote, 'The shittiest he's ever seen in his entire career.'" She pauses. "And he had his I'm-not-joking-look. I can't afford to fail this."

"I can't afford it either." My eyes dance back to the corner of the room, where Svetlana is now

asking Em to perform an arabesque for her. Once Emilia's body is arched, Svetlana pushes her foot.

"You're not supposed to move. Your body is in the movement, and your face cannot be that serious all the time. You're falling in love, your story is only starting."

Jen snaps her fingers. "Come on, Nick. Eduardo gave us thirty minutes to work on the wedding choreography. He told me to step it up, and that he didn't want to feel like he was looking at our funerals."

Svetlana raises her voice. "Okay, enough for today. You need to clear your mind and come back tomorrow with more power and determination."

"I should stay and watch Jen."

Svetlana takes a deep breath—she rarely gets annoyed, but when she does, she can be scary. Clearly, she wants to calm herself down. "I think it's best you review some of the videos and you'll be back at it tomorrow."

"Okay." Em's voice cracks. And she walks past us without a glance, her head and shoulders high, but her chin is quivering and her eyes brim with tears.

I step toward her but Jen holds me back. "Listen, I know it sucks. And I feel bad for her too. But we have to rehearse. If you think Svetlana was hard on her, imagine Svetlana and Eduardo together yelling at us that we're not worth the paper the showcase program is printed on." She stares at me. "This is our last chance to show the world we're worth it before graduation."

ALWAYS SECOND BEST

I look at the door one second longer, before turning back to Jen. "Okay, let's do this, but you better give it your all too."

"I always do," she replies.

And we jump. And we glide. And we do pirouette after pirouette.

When Eduardo comes back and watches us, he's still unhappy. Apparently, we need to believe in the story more. Instead of leaving rehearsal at seven, we end up staying until nine.

My entire body is killing me. Jen seems exhausted.

"I'm going to stay a bit longer," she says and Svetlana nods.

Eduardo is out of the door without a backward glance at us, but Svetlana tilts her head. "I know it's not easy. But you two have what it takes. Don't forget that." And she heads out.

"I'm going to go check on Em. Are you sure you don't want to grab something to eat?"

"No. Not right now. I need to practice my *relevé*. I can never quite get it perfect."

I don't see any issues with her *relevé*, but I know Jen enough to know that I won't get her to change her mind.

I head out of the rehearsal room and text Em. Are you okay? Do you want to meet up? I need a shower and I need food.

Em: I'm fine. You must be exhausted. I'll see you tomorrow. Love you. ☺ ☺ ☺

Nick: Are you sure?

Em: I am. I want to continue watching the videos from last year's showcase, and the rehearsal one from last week. And you should go to bed. I know you're exhausted.

I'm barely able to walk, but I don't want her going to bed sad.

My phone buzzes again. Em: I promise I'll be fine. I'll see you tomorrow. <3

Nick: Okay. I'll see you at breakfast. I love you.

CHAPTER 29 – EM

SEEING THE WORDS "I love you" on my phone from Nick still brings out a rush of emotions. Because I know he means it. Because I love him too. Because even though I had a bad day he still manages to make me smile.

I pause the video of last year's showcase. Watching them has definitely taught me one thing: I do suck.

Svetlana is pushing me to be better. But, can I be better? Or have I reached the point of no return?

I stretch. The room is dark and I rub my eyes. Jen's not back yet. Maybe she's still practicing. If I can watch the way she creates the emotions, I could probably get better.

I change into my tights and a tank top, grab my bag that has my pointes and march out of the room. I'm a girl with a mission. And my mission is not to fail miserably when everyone has put so much hope on me, when so much money has been spent on me, when people believe in me.

I push the door of the studio open and Jen's in the middle of the room, repeating the same pirouette followed by a *relevé* again and again. She stops and turns to me. "What are you doing here?"

"I thought I'd watch you and try to work on the first choreography again."

Jen lowers her arms and narrows her eyes, biting the skin of her finger. "Really?"

"I need to be better."

"We all do." Jen sighs. "But you have to remember that they chose you as an understudy for a reason."

"Because they took pity on me?"

"Are you kidding? We're in the ballet world. This is not charity." She takes a step forward. "They chose you because you showed the most promise. And if you showed the most promise, it's because you also managed to evoke some emotions while you were dancing. Right now, you look like every turn, every *fouetté*, every *grand jeté* is the end of the world. You're not supposed to be Emilia Moretti when you dance."

"I know that."

"I've told you before that I don't think you're dancing for the right reasons. But honestly, If you're here, though, why not make the best of it by giving it your all?" She shrugs as if she holds that same speech with herself every single day. "Let's work on your choreography."

"Why would you do that?"

ALWAYS SECOND BEST

"Because, right now, I feel like I'm losing ground and I think rehearsing with you might be helpful. Maybe…and if you tell anybody I told you this, I would deny it, but maybe I can learn from you."

I raise an eyebrow and she laughs. "You never know."

I put on my pointes and rise to my toes. "Let's do this."

And for the next two hours, we rehearse side by side, only talking to tell the other what we think they should improve, and how to improve it.

We might not be best friends, but when we leave the studio, I feel like we've found new respect for one another.

CHAPTER 30 - NICK

THE PAST WEEK has been full of rehearsals, and even though Jen seemed to be optimistic at the beginning, Eduardo's criticism has taken its toll. While Em's been dancing better and better, Jen's been making more mistakes.

But to me, it looks like Em's trying to force herself to enjoy dancing. She's not smiling when she manages to do an entire routine without any mistakes. She's not smiling when Svetlana praises her, and she's not smiling when her mom calls her to check in on her. At times, she glances up as if she's having silent conversations with herself. And I know that's her way of checking in with her Nonna, thinking about what she would say, what advice she would give.

I know she hasn't been talking to her dad for at least a week and an half. She didn't even go home last weekend. Today, she's rehearsing with the rest of the showcase, while Jen and I get to have a private session with Eduardo and Svetlana.

ALWAYS SECOND BEST

"One more time," Eduardo says. I've only had two classes with him and he's always seemed genuinely interested in the students, but right now he sounds more like a drill sergeant.

Jen catches her breath. "Okay."

We've been rehearsing for more than two hours, but it's still not enough. We're not perfect. We're far from perfect.

We do the routine again and Svetlana catches my eyes, she shakes her head, purses her lip. Both she and Eduardo whisper to one another. "Enough for today, it's already late. But I want to see you both on Sunday afternoon. All next week, we have group rehearsal, but you two are not yet ready to shine."

They leave the room, and even though they don't slam the door behind them, it's not a happy exit.

"You need to keep your arms in the air for a second longer," I tell Jen for what seems like the thousandth time.

"No I don't," she replies.

"Yes, you do. Why don't you listen to me?" I can't help but sounding annoyed.

"What's up your butt?" she asks and steps closer to me. "You've been on edge all week. And honestly, it's getting tiresome."

"If you would listen to what I'm trying to tell you, I wouldn't need to be on edge like I am."

"I am listening." She raises both hands in the air. "But are you paying attention to what you're saying? You give me one direction and then change it five minutes later. Svetlana..."

"Svetlana isn't going to be in the audience writing for the *New York Times*."

"You're right. But I'm pretty sure she knows what she's talking about."

"Why do you have to argue?"

"Why do you have to be so bossy? I don't know how Em manages to not kill you."

"Let's do the entire scene again. One more time."

"No," she replies and turns away.

"What do you mean no?"

"I mean, no!" She softens her tone. "I mean, let's go and take a break and maybe even walk outside for five minutes."

"If I mess this up, my dad is never going to support me."

"I've had it!" She huffs. "What do you want?" She nudges me. "What do you effing want?"

"What do you want? You're dancing like you're not even believing in it. You're dancing like a fucking robot with no feelings!"

And I want to take those words back. She gasps and then shakes her head.

"Whatever, Nicholas. What-fuck-ever. I'm dancing like a robot with no feelings? You're dancing like you're trying to please everyone but yourself!"

"Right back at you."

"Great comeback!"

We both stare into each other's eyes and I won't back down first. I won't look away. "Why did you even join the School?"

"Because I'm good at it. Because I enjoy it. Because I'm made for it."

"You're supposed to want it," I reply and Em enters the room at this moment. She glances from me to Jen and frowns. But she frowns at me, not at Jen, and that throws me off my game. A little.

"I wanted to join the School because I didn't know what else to do. I don't know what else to do but dance. I dance to live. I live to dance. I dance to exist. If I don't dance, no one sees me, no one ever cares. But that's not important to me. Dancing makes me happy and I can make other people happy with dancing too. Why are you even dancing? Except for getting into Em's tutu." She coughs. "No offense, Em."

"None taken," Em replies, and she looks at me with pursed lips and her air that says I've gone too far.

I know I have, I shouldn't let out my anger on Jen. She's working hard. We're all working hard. I step forward. "I'm sorry. I'm stressed, that's all."

"We're all stressed and I know I need to up my game, or they're going to call on Em to dance for me and that'd be the worse day of my life." She coughs again. "No offense, Em."

"Again, none taken. I know you have issues expressing your feelings and all." Em waves her hand in front of her as if to dismiss what Jen said.

"Why don't you take a break?" I ask Jen.

And she nods and I notice now that her foot's bleeding so hard there's some on the floor. "Are you okay?"

"It's fine. My toes are bothering me, but nothing major." She heads out. "I'll see you tomorrow morning, first thing."

"On Saturday?"

"You said we needed to practice and you're right. And Em? Don't forget our number one rule."

"Don't worry, I won't. See you later, Jen."

She closes the door behind her, limping. And Em turns to me, her hands on her hips. "You need to chill."

"I'm on edge."

"Again, we all are. That's not a reason to talk to Jen like this."

"I never would have thought you'd defend her."

"Tell me about it," she sighs. "We've been talking. A bit. She has good moments."

I step to her, kiss her lips. She's in jeans and a V-neck shirt and I can see her bra straps. They're black and suddenly, I don't really care much about Jen. I deepen the kiss, until I feel her melt in my arms. "Let's go out," I blurt out and her eyes widen.

"And go where?"

"To my place to play video games, or Central Park or maybe we could go see a movie or something."

"Aren't you supposed to go out with Rob tonight?" she asks, kissing my neck.

"True. But I'm sure he wouldn't mind you coming with us," I tell her.

"You're probably right, but I promised Mom I'd go home for dinner tonight."

"I'd ask if you want me to come with you, but I'm pretty sure the answer is no."

"Well, it's my first dinner back at home since Nonna's funeral and the first time I'll see my dad."

I kiss her again. "Call me or Rob if you need anything, promise?"

"Promise," she replies and I take her hand in mine. Together, we leave the room, and together I feel like we're stronger.

CHAPTER 31 – EM

SAYING GOODBYE to Nick always takes forever, but it's a good forever, it's a forever I never want to end. But I know I can't be late for dinner. I enter my dorm room, which Jen has started to decorate a little, like she finally feels a bit more at home in it, but she hasn't put up any pictures. She did add a few pillows here and there from her old dorm room. And she put up two posters on her side of the room: one of Paris at night and another one showing bleeding feet in pointes. Fitting for her today. We still talk about Natalya, and we still haven't heard anything from her directly.

I know she's seen my message I sent her on Facebook, but she hasn't replied.

I only need to get my bag and then I'm out of the School. Mom texted me again to remind me about tonight. Like it's the first time ever I go home to see them. Like I haven't seen them in years. Like we're almost strangers.

Jen is pretty neat and the room is definitely organized, so I notice right away the envelope on my desk.

Note to self: don't get your hopes too high.

This might be a letter from one of our grandaunts in the South, or maybe simply an ad or a flyer. It might be for Jen. It might be anything. Or it might be everything.

I pick it up slowly, not recognizing the handwriting. My hand shakes as I open it.

Dear Emilia,

I'm sorry I did not write back earlier. And I'm very sorry about the way I acted back in August. I've received both your letters and it took me that long to have the courage to write you back.

I only want you to know that giving you up for adoption was not an easy decision and that it was complicated.

Maybe in the future, we could exchange letters again. I am not supposed to talk to you or visit you or anything. But know that I was there last year at the showcase and I'll be there again this year. I've followed your progress and even though it hurts to see you and to know you must hate me, I'm really happy that you're happy. I do mean that.

All the very best, and again, I'm so sorry.
Claire.

ALWAYS SECOND BEST

I clutch the letter in my hand; I'm not sure if I'm breathing at all. It feels like I'm not. She left a phone number at the bottom.

Should I call her? Should I wait? What would I say?

My phone rings, distracting me from my thoughts. "Hi Mom," I say.

"Are you on your way? I wanted to let you know I made a molten lava cake." She pauses. "Well, I didn't make it. But I bought it and the guy who sold it to me told me it was the best in all of Brooklyn. Of course, unless you don't want to eat lava cake because you're rehearsing."

"I can't wait for the lava cake, Mom."

"So, we'll see you soon?"

"Of course. I'm on my way."

"Okay, honey." And she sounds relieved. I carefully place the letter in my wallet and head out.

Dinner with my parents never felt this excruciating.

The table is set for three, but Dad isn't there. He's not there when I enter the house, when Mom hugs me, when we sit down.

There's a lingering burned smell in the small dining room. Mom's never been a pro at cooking and always said how happy she was Nonna owned a restaurant. She's got bags under her eyes and her black dress emphasizes her pale complexion.

"Your father had to work," she says. But she doesn't believe it. She looks exactly the same way as when Roberto and I told her we weren't the ones who plugged the toilet with candy wraps when we were about five and seven years old.

"He works a lot."

"He's gone a lot. I think that's his way of dealing with Nonna's passing." She settles at the table and passes me the loaf of herb bread. "How are you doing?"

"I'm doing okay. I've been spending some time with Nick, and Jen isn't half bad after all."

"That's good. I'm glad to hear you have people surrounding you." Mom clears her throat and glances at Dad's empty seat.

And I feel terrible for not checking up on her last week. "I could come by on Tuesday if you want. Tuesdays are usually easier for me."

"I know you're busy, sweetie. Don't worry. I'm fine. I really am. I miss your Nonna, that's all. She was really amazing and an inspiration." Mom bites her upper lip. Her own parents died a long time ago, and she always told Nonna that she was happy to have found another family.

"So, tell me, are you reopening the restaurant or what did you decide?"

"I'm not sure yet. It's not decided." She tries to smile. "But anyways, tell me more about your school, about preparing for the showcase. I'm so proud of all your hard work."

"It's definitely not easy and I don't think I'll have much to show this year. I mean, I'd understand if you decided not to come."

ALWAYS SECOND BEST

"Are you kidding? Of course we want to be there." Her eyes widen and she looks at me carefully. "You do know that I'm proud of you, right?"

"Mmm-hmm."

"There's no 'hmm.' We are proud of you. For your hard work, but also for who you're becoming. You care about others, you try your best."

"But I'm never first."

"You are. You are first. With people and you should be first with yourself." She bites into her burned macaroni and cheese and grimaces. "This is quite awful. I could order pizza."

"I'm sure it's fine." And this time when I smile, it comes more easily. Mom does love me. And she's proud of me. And maybe I can learn to be proud of me too. Even if I'm not first.

CHAPTER 32 – NICK

ROB ARRIVES AT my parents' house ten minutes late, which is nothing. I'm usually always at least fifteen minutes late, except Rob's always early. It's one of the things he tells me actually annoys him about Giovanni. Giovanni can't be on time to save his life.

"Hey," Rob says and he looks like shit. He's way too pale, his hair is all over the place and he walks as if it's painful to move.

"Are you okay?"

"Fine, totally fine." He shivers. "Still recovering from that stupid cold." He leans against the wall. "Is everything moving or is that me?"

He's sliding down as if he's about to faint and my heart races. I squat down. "Come on, Rob. What's wrong?" He doesn't answer. I stand back up. "Mom?" My voice is higher pitched than usual. And Dad pokes his head out of his office that's down the hallway.

"She went to visit Meaghan. What's going on?"

ALWAYS SECOND BEST

Great. Rob's about to pass out here and Mom's out with a friend. What's my dad going to do? Tell me he shouldn't be there in the first place?

"What's Rob doing here?" he asks, but he sounds more confused than angry. Maybe because Rob's on the floor.

"I don't think Rob's doing well."

"I'm fine," Rob says, but then he starts coughing and coughing and coughing.

Dad strides our way. Even though it's Friday evening, he's working. He and Mom still haven't missed one single appointment with Dr. Grahams though, so somehow therapy must be working.

"You don't seem fine at all." Dad touches Rob's forehead and the crease between his eyebrows deepens.

Rob's swaying and there's sweat around his nose. His hands shake.

Dad turns to me. "Call 911. Now. I'll call Dr. Wicks at the hospital and tell him to meet us there immediately."

"I can't. Health insurance. Not." Rob can barely talk, and it seems he's getting worse by the second.

My heart pounds and my entire body buzzes. I call 911 while Dad holds Rob by the waist, talking to him about his classes, about Giovanni, about Emilia. Rob doesn't answer. He nods from time to time but his eyes don't focus.

"What's your emergency?"

"My friend has been sick and I don't know, it looks like he's fainting." Dad gestures for me to give him the phone, and for once his taking-charge attitude

doesn't annoy me. I hand the phone over to him. And sit next to Rob. I've never seen him like this, I've never seen anyone like this. "You're going to be okay," I whisper, but there's a voice inside of me that screams *what if he's not?* Telling it to shut up seems to make it even louder, so I concentrate on listening to what Dad's saying.

"It's a young man—eighteen years old. It seems he's been sick and he's losing consciousness. He's having trouble breathing."

Dad glances at me and he squeezes my shoulder. It's quick but it's there, and it scares the shit out of me. What is Dad talking about? Rob's breathing fine.

"Rob?" I call. But Rob isn't answering. "Rob, come on, don't be an ass."

Dad shakes his head, whispers, "It's okay, son. Help is coming."

And then he talks into the phone again. "I don't know if he's been taking anything." He gives our address to the dispatcher and nods as he follows the instructions. "We're waiting. Yes."

It only takes a few seconds to hear the sirens and soon our front door opens. Men and one woman enter, take control, put an oxygen mask on Rob's face. "Is he going to be okay? He's going to be okay, right?"

"Do you want to come with us to the hospital?" the woman asks my father and my father nods, pushing me with him.

"We'll both come."

His work cell phone rings and for the first time in years, he totally ignores it.

ALWAYS SECOND BEST

Instead, he grabs his personal iPhone. "Hi, we're arriving at Hospital North in about two minutes. They're putting Rob under ventilation and they're talking about his body going into shock. I don't know what he has or what's going on. Yes, the crew is here and we're about to go in the ambulance. Thank you, David."

I turn to Rob and his eyes are closed, his body is surrounded by people and he has a mask on his face, things in his arms. We should have taken a helicopter, we should have done something else, something sooner.

"You're going to be okay, Rob," I whisper and my father puts his hand on my shoulder again.

"They're taking good care of him."

I stare at Rob's ashen face; the beeps are getting louder and louder.

"He's not going to die, right?" I ask without looking at my father.

"They're doing their best. Rob is young." My father uses his no-nonsense tone, which I know is usually a way for him to present the facts, but his hand is on my shoulder and he squeezes it. "They're doing their best," he repeats.

My hands clam up. He didn't answer my question.

Rob can't die.

He can't die.

CHAPTER 33 – EM

AFTER DINNER AT MOM'S, I go back to the dorms, almost expecting Rob and Nick to be there waiting for me, asking me to join them, like they used to last year. But there's no one. Jen isn't there either. I take Claire's letter out from my wallet and reread it. Again. Maybe I should call her. But not before telling Mom and Dad about it. I couldn't tonight. Mom's too fragile right now and Dad's too absent.

My phone rings and my lips stretch into a smile when I see Nick's number. "Missing me already?" I joke.

"You have to come to the hospital. Your parents are on their way. My dad called them."

"What are you talking about?"

"It's about Rob."

ALWAYS SECOND BEST

That doesn't make any sense. My brain isn't registering. Rob's fine. "Rob's fine," I repeat out loud. "You guys went to play video games. He's fine."

"He came to my house and he blacked out, lost consciousness. They said he stopped breathing."

"Oh my god! Where are you?' My voice rises.

"North Hospital," he replies and I keep him on the phone as I rush out. "My dad sent his driver for you. He's waiting in front of the school."

"How are my parents going to get there?"

"He called another car for them."

"Okay. Okay." I see the black sedan Nick's father uses, the one that picked us up on the Fourth of July. The driver opens the door for me, and he's not smiling. Does he know? Is it his usual look? Why am I not at the hospital yet?

"Em?" Nick calls my name as if he tried already a few times. "Are you there?"

"I'm in the car. What did the doctors say? What happened?" I know I sound panicky but I can't help myself. I can't lose Rob. We can't lose Rob. Rob is going to be fine. He's going to cure diseases and get married and adopt a kid or two. Like he said he would when he turns thirty. That's his ten-year plan, as he calls it. He's going to be fine.

"My father's talking to his friend, I haven't heard anything yet."

"Stay with me on the phone, please."

"Of course." And he stays with me until the driver pulls in front of the hospital.

When I get out of the car, my heart hurts and pounds and it's hard to breathe.

Nick's at the entrance, and I fall into him. "Where is he? What's going on?"

"He's in an intensive station," he says. The words tumble out of his mouth and he tightens his embrace as if holding me is the only thing that makes sense. "He came to play video games tonight, but he was really sick so we came here."

"I need to see him," I whisper. "I need to see him." Nick lets me go but his fingers find mine as we rush inside.

He explains the doctors won't let anyone see him. My parents are on their way. Brooklyn is a bit farther away, that's why it's taking longer for them. The hospital's full of people and when we pass through the first reception area to the second one, the families have more tears, more anxiety rippling through the way they sit on the hard gray chairs, or the way they hold on to one another.

Nick's father's talking to a tall, lanky man in scrubs. He's rubbing the back of his neck. Like his son. And like Nick, it's his tell—something's not going well.

My heart drops further down and my hands clam up.

"What's going on?" I step to Nick's dad and he turns to me. His mouth gapes open and I've never seen him so taken aback; his hand reaches up to my shoulder and he pulls me into a hug. A hug that feels like nothing will ever be the same.

And panic rises in my chest. Strong and steady panic that rushes inside of me. "What's going on?" I whisper.

"We need to wait for your parents," he answers and gently lets me go, keeping a hand on my shoulder as if to ground me. "This is Dr. Wicks," he introduces me. "He's a good friend of mine. He knows your dad. He's taking good care of your brother, I promise."

"I want to see him."

"I'm sorry, but you can't see him yet. And again, I need to wait for your parents to arrive."

"I'm his sister!" I glance at my feet and then back at the doctor, my voice barely above a whisper. "I'm his sister," I repeat and it hits me full force: I am his sister. And nothing will ever change that. And I hope he knows it, that I made it clear enough, that he doesn't think he's not good enough.

Nick's father uses his calm voice—his soothing voice—to talk to me. "Why don't you sit with Nick until your parents arrive?"

I don't want to sit. But then there's a shuffle on the other side of the room, someone's rushed between the revolving doors and Dr. Wicks frowns. "I have to go. But I'll be back. I promise you I'm going to take the best possible care of your brother." And he strides away from me.

Nick's father lets go of my shoulder, but he leans in toward me. He's as tall as Nick, and they have the same ocean eyes. Except his are full of storms. "I promise you, Emilia. I'll make sure Roberto gets the best care. I promise."

"Why would you do that?" I ask, wanting to bite my tongue for sounding a bit ungrateful or

doubtful, but it's not like Nick's father has been very welcoming to us for the past few months. "I can't lose him too," I say and my voice is small. I'm not even sure he heard the second part.

"I know you can't." He rubs the back of his neck again. "I'm sorry if I put you...if we put you in the middle of our business. I know it's not your fault. It's just...parents always want the best for their kids."

And I'm not the best for his son.

I turn away. Everything's too much, too painful, too scary.

I feel the tears on my face and I want to hold them in, to bury them back inside, but I can't.

Everything's blurry and I don't hear him or anyone anymore.

I want my brother. I want my grandmother. I want to talk to them again. I want my brother to walk out of this door and tell me it was all a prank, that nothing has changed, and I want Nonna to bring food to the hospital like she would, because she always said food helps everything.

"Emilia," Nick's father calls my name. Maybe for the second or third time. "I'm sorry. About everything."

CHAPTER 34 - NICK

MY FATHER'S PHONE RANG and this time, he apparently has to take it. He squeezes my shoulder once before heading out.

I take Em's hand in mine. It feels cold and she doesn't look at me. She's sniffling and I want to scream. I want to stop the world for a second and reset it to the first time we noticed Rob wasn't doing well. I want to bring him to the doctors then. I want to make sure he's going to be okay.

Rob's my best friend.

Em clutches my hand and I clutch it back.

I swallow my sobs because right now, right here, I feel helpless, and I feel so fucking young and so fucking old at once.

CHAPTER 35- EM

"WHERE IS HE?" Mom rushes through the door, her eyes haggard and her hair all over the place. "Where is he?" she repeats. She's still wearing the black dress she had on for dinner, but it's all wrinkly.

Dad follows her. His eyes dart everywhere, landing on Nick.

"What did you do?" he yells and everyone turns our way. The lady who was softly crying on one of the chairs stops and stares at my dad.

"Dino," Mom says, but there's no stopping him.

He strides to Nick. "Where's my son?"

Nick gets up and puts a calming hand on my father's arm, but that only seems to enrage him even more.

"Do not dare touch me. You soil everything you touch. Like your father," he shouts. He curls his hands into fists and I want to put myself between them, but Mom holds me back.

"Dino, leave Nick alone," she says again and two nurses head our way, shaking their heads.

Nick opens his mouth, but then his eyes find mine and he steps away. Away from my father, the situation, the drama.

"Listen to me when I talk. Don't be a coward. Your father took everything from me. Everything! My career, my life. Everything! You will not take my daughter and my son away from me!"

Who is this man? Who is this man red from anger and not caring about anyone's feelings but his own?

"You are going to need to leave," one of the nurses tells him. She's a petite black woman, but the way she stares at my dad tells me she means business. "You will not disturb the people on this floor, not the patients. If you want to fight, take it outside."

My dad deflates and falls on a nearby chair, his shoulders slouched. "How is my son? I want to see my son."

Mom wraps her arm around me and together we walk to where he's sitting. She sits next to my dad without a word.

The nurse puts a compassionate hand on her shoulder. "The doctor will be right with you."

Mom's lips quiver, but she keeps her chin high and nods. As if one meltdown was the only one our family could endure.

I go to Nick and hug him. "Maybe it's best if you leave," I say. Even though I need him. Even though he gives me strength. Even though he makes

everything less scary. "I don't want my dad to lose his temper on you. I don't want that for you and I don't want that for Rob. I don't want my dad to say something he won't be able to take back or make amends for."

"Will you call me as soon as you hear something?" he whispers into my hair. I nod and he tightens his arms around my waist. "Rob's a fighter. He's going to be fine."

And I'm not sure if he's trying to convince me or himself.

CHAPTER 36 - NICK

I'VE NEVER FELT so helpless in my fucking life. And I've never felt so scared or so angry or so in need of punching someone.

I could go home. I could try yet again to talk to my father. I could actually thank him for taking care of Rob, for making sure he's got the best care.

But right now I can't do what everyone's expecting me to do. My feet take me back to the School of Performing Arts. And I head straight to the upstairs studio. There's music playing inside of it and Jen's rehearsing. The same movement. Again and again. But with so much passion and dedication.

I watch her from the door until the music stops. She turns to me, out of breath. "I didn't think anyone was as crazy as me. It's almost eleven p.m. on Friday—aren't you supposed to be out with your girlfriend?" She sounds genuinely curious, as if seeing me there doesn't make any sense.

"I used to rehearse every night too."

"I know you did. But that was when you wanted to prove something to someone else. I only want to prove something to myself." She shrugs. "Natalya understood me the best. We never really talked, but I knew exactly how she felt."

"Dancing's my life."

"Yes it is, but it's not the only thing making you breathe, waking you up. It's your passion. I see it, I see how much you love it and how you're going to have a wonderful career, but it's going to be only that for you."

I want to protest but I know she's right. Dancing is in my blood. Dancing's my passion, and it is a big part of me, but it isn't the only part.

Jen slides past me. "The room's all yours."

I grab my iPod and tune it in to one of the latest more modern musical pieces. I take off my shoes and my sweatshirt and I let the music guide me.

I dance.

I dance for hours, until my entire mind is consumed by the music, the story, the movements, the emotions. Until I'm consumed by the dance.

But as soon as the music stops—as soon as I step back into reality—it hits me right in the face. Rob's at the hospital. I wipe my forehead and breathe deeply.

I hurry to check my cell phone. Em hasn't called, but she did text.

Dr. Wicks told us Rob's appendix had ruptured. He almost died. Still in surgery.

I reply:

ALWAYS SECOND BEST

Thinking about you. Call me as soon as you hear something.

After taking a short shower, I check again. Still nothing. I'm tempted to call her, but the hospital doesn't allow cell phones in the waiting area.

I text my father—based on our text history, the last time I did was for his birthday five months ago. And he hadn't even replied. "I've been trying to reach Em. Any news from Rob?"

My cell buzzes right away. "They're trying to stabilize him and then he needs to go to surgery. His appendix almost exploded. I'm in the cafeteria with Em's father right now." Why are they together again? Funny how they both seem to think we all need to stay apart, but they're spending almost more time together now than when they worked together. My phone buzzes again. "Em's with her mom, still in the waiting area. I'll keep you updated."

There's nothing I can do.

Except wait.

CHAPTER 37 - EM

MINUTES FEEL LIKE THE HOURS before an audition. They go by way too slowly. Right after the doctor told us that Roberto had blood poisoning following a burst appendix, Dad went with Nick's father to the cafeteria for thirty minutes. When they came back, Nick's dad was frowning even more and Dad's scowl was even bigger.

Dad and Mom haven't exchanged a word ever since Dad yelled at Nick, but they did hold one another when the doctor talked to them. He said he would keep us updated as regularly as possible

I shift on my seat and I glance at the bathroom sign but I don't move. Instead, I focus my attention on the people in the waiting area.

Some have come and gone. The lady who was crying left with a smile, but the people who were smiling left sobbing.

I'm not sure what to think, or what to hope for. I'm afraid to jinx anything. I'm afraid to strike a deal with a God I'm not even sure I believe in. I'm afraid to see the doctor come back and afraid he's never going to come back.

The nurses at the desk are talking about their kids—the one who gave my father the calm-down look has a little boy who's staying with her mother tonight. They continue to tend to the people arriving, continue to check behind the closed door. I wonder how they do it. Caring for patients in the emergency room, seeing the misery and sadness of their families, friends, loved ones, and still going home and managing to continue taking care of others.

"I need to ask what's going on," Mom finally says, and jumps to her feet. She pulls her hair into a ponytail and without a backward glance at my dad, she heads to the nurses' station. "The doctor said he was going to come back to update us. It's been an hour already since he told us that. Do you know if our son is still in surgery?"

"Let me see what's going on," the nurse named Mandy says.

"Thank you, thank you."

She picks up the phone and after a few seconds of nodding and "yes sir," she purses her lips. "Dr. Wicks is sorry it has taken him so long. Can you and your family please follow me?"

Mom gestures to Dad to get up and pulls me by the hand. "Of course."

The nurse opens the doors with her badge and brings us to a small room. We pass patients in bed, another door at the end of the hallway that looks like the entrance to operating rooms.

Dr. Wicks enters only a few seconds later. He looks more worried than the last time I saw him, more shaken.

"Mr. and Mrs. Moretti, as I've told you. Roberto developed sepsis. If your friends had not brought him to the ER, he would have died."

Mom gasps and Dad leans against the wall. My insides twist because based on the way Dr. Wicks is now clearing his throat, it seems we're not hearing the end of the story.

"He has a very bad bacterial infection, which not only affected his lungs but also his kidneys. We're trying to save them but he might need a kidney transplant."

Dad perks up in his chair. "We can give one, right. As his parents?"

"If it comes to that, yes, you will definitely be considered."

Dad breathes hard and Mom's crying softly. He stares at her for a second, before asking, "If he needs a kidney transplant, and we're not a match, what would happen?"

"He could live on dialysis for a while. He'd be on the transplant list."

"He's planning to travel. He's going to receive a prize and he's going to go to Europe, to Geneva and to London. He's going to learn with the best of the bests."

"He will need to take it easy for a bit, and it all depends on how we can manage his infection and how he recovers from the treatment we've given him. There is damage but it may not come to that point. The next forty-eight hours will be crucial," the doctor explains.

ALWAYS SECOND BEST

And Dad's eyes evade mine to fall on Mom again. He whispers, "I'm sorry," and then says, "Emilia should be tested too."

I nod. Roberto and I might not be blood related, but if there's any chance I could help him here I'm in, no questions asked.

"I've understood she wasn't related by blood. Of course, we'll test her, but it's a bit more complicated since she's a minor, and the chances are very low anyway."

"You don't understand. You have to test her. You have to make sure Roberto is going to be okay. And I don't care if I lose everything. I don't care if I lose everyone. I can't be responsible for Roberto missing out on life." His voice breaks with each word. He closes his eyes. "Emilia needs to be tested too. Because she's my daughter too. She's Roberto's half-sister."

The entire room stops buzzing. I'm not sure if everyone stopped talking or if I'm blocking them out. I stare at Dad, then at Mom, whose mouth gapes open.

It can't be true.

Mom's face turns even paler and she clutches my shoulder so hard I wince. "Roberto is our son. And Emilia's been adopted. She can't be his half-sister. She's his sister. But not his half-sister." She turns to Dad. Her hand falls from my shoulder but she's not letting go. She holds on to my hand as if she's afraid I'm going to disappear.

"She's his half-sister," he repeats and he stares right ahead, not moving.

"I don't understand," I say. His words don't register. They don't compute.

"What are you saying?" Mom blurts—her words tangled into one high pitch. "It doesn't make sense." She stares at our joined hands and then bores her eyes into Dad's. "Dino, what are you saying?" she repeats.

"It was one night. One mistake. And when she told me she was pregnant..." Dad's tone is apologetic. He glances down at the floor, but then looks at Mom with so much despair in his eyes that I almost feel sorry for him.

Mom shrieks. "She's my daughter. I don't care what you're saying. Why did you do that to us? You lied to us! You lied to me, you lied to her! You lied to everyone!" And then she takes a deep breath, her hand squeezes mine and she turns my face to her. There are tears in her eyes. "Everything is going to be okay. None of this is your fault. I love you." Her voice only slightly quivers.

I'm numb and nod. I don't want her to cry. I don't want her to be sad and there's a sour taste in my mouth.

"You...you're my father." My voice sounds as hollow as my chest.

The doctor clears his throat. And there's pity in the way he looks at all of us. I even forgot he was standing right here. "I can give you some time."

"You said there was only a little time," I reply.

"Can she get tested too?" Dad asks the doctor. There's a mixture of hope and sadness in his voice.

"We will test her, of course—if neither of you are compatible and if it comes to it. We're still trying

to save his kidneys. He's still in the operating room. And you can wait here if you'd like. There's a vending machine in the hallway."

"I can't stay in the same room as him," Mom says and stands up. "I can't stay in the same room. I can't look at him." Her voice is shaking. Her hands are shaking. Her entire body is shaking.

And I don't know what to do. I don't know what to say. I don't know where to look, who to follow, whether I heard everything correctly or not.

That's not possible.

My life can't be a lie. My entire life cannot be a lie. It's like my father's words are slowly making their way through my brain. *I am Roberto's half-sister. He is my birth father.*

The doctor steps forward, and he deserves an Oscar or something: he's collected and cool, like he sees this every single day.

"You can wait in an adjacent room. Let me show you where it is. Know that I'm doing my best for your son and brother."

"Emilia, come with me," she says, stretching her hand out to me. "If you want. You can stay here and talk to your father. I'd understand." She's breathing in and out deeply, almost like she's counting in her head to try to calm herself down. Dad's plopped on a chair, his shoulders slouched.

"Dad?" I ask.

He puts his face in his hands. Like he can't believe what happened.

I can't believe it either.

"Why?" I'm surprised how clear my voice is. "Why didn't you tell us? Why didn't you say anything last year, last summer? I actually thought about it as a possibility, but then I told myself my father would never lie to my mother like this. He would never put us through this." I wait for an answer that doesn't come. "I'm not sure what to think anymore. And you know what's funny? I thought knowing where I came from would make everything easier. It doesn't. Right now it's harder than it's ever been."

"Emilia," my dad whispers. "Emilia, I'm sorry."

"I think you should apologize to Mom."

Mom's still standing in the room. It looks like she's ready to jump in the middle to protect me.

His eyes dart over to her but then he looks at the ceiling. "You have no idea the pressure I've been under. How many times I simply wanted to tell you everything." His words tumble out. "I got fired because I embezzled money. I got fired because I did things I was not supposed to do."

Mom gasps.

"I'm not done. I have something else to tell you." He's slouching even more. Lost in his own world. "Since it's all out, since everything is already said and done. Since I already lost everything and everyone."

I sigh. I'm half tempted to take Mom's hand and rush out of the room, half tempted to sit by him, to ask him to tell me it's not true, or to look at him and see if I can find myself in him. We've got the same skin color, though mine is a tinge darker, kind of like Poppa's was. We don't have anything else in common...except our eyes. We have the same stupid

brown eyes. He's whispering to himself again. "I lost everything."

I crouch next to him. "One thing I've learned is that you only lose if you don't fight. Nonna always said that too, and she was right."

He bores his eyes into mine. "You have a twin sister."

CHAPTER 38 - NICK

I STILL HAVEN'T HEARD ANYTHING from Emilia. And Dad said he hasn't seen her in a few hours. Apparently, there was a fight at the hospital. But he didn't want to tell me more.

Kayode hugged me when I came into the dorm room, and he's been quiet all evening. As if he knows I need some time for myself. He went to bed almost an hour ago.

The warm spring weather from the past couple days has turned to shit and the rain doesn't stop pouring. The noise it makes on our dorm windows would prevent anyone from sleeping, but Kayode is still softly snoring.

I toss and toss and toss, but that has nothing to do with the rain.

I'm worried about Rob.

I'm worried about Em.

And I'm worried about me and my decisions and my desire to always butt heads with my father. It

was almost simple to have him question every decision I ever made, because I knew how to fight back. I don't want to be a lawyer. That much is clear, and I want to dance—that much is also clear.

But I don't think I want to join a company. At least not yet. I might prefer helping others, rather than dancing professionally myself. I could go to one of the best dancing programs and combine it with an education degree. I could at least check more about it. I loved showing Em how to create the emotions. And not only because it allowed me to get closer to her, but because seeing the expression on her face when she succeeded was so rewarding.

I toss around again.

I've been working on that one goal for the past fifteen years, ever since Mom convinced Dad that it was okay to take me to a dance class at the local studio. Ever since I felt like I could conquer the world in one leap. Ever since Dad told me it was only a hobby.

If I don't achieve this goal, does it mean I failed? Or does it mean something else entirely?

Standing up to Dad should have made everything easier.

There's a soft knock at our door. Almost too soft to be heard over Kayode's snores.

Almost too soft to not be part of my imagination.

But someone knocks again.

"We all know it's for you," Kayode mutters. "So, why don't you move your cute little ass to the door so the rest of us, aka me, can get a few hours of snooze before tomorrow?"

"I'm going, I'm going." I jump down and open the door.

Em rushes into my arms—sniffling, but not crying. I'm not sure if she's all cried out or if she's trying to be strong.

I hold her for a second before Kayode voices the fears I can't express. "Oh my God, Em, is it Roberto? Is he okay?"

Em nods into my shoulder before pulling back a little. "He's fine. He's out of surgery and in recovery. They think they got everything out but they're not entirely sure. They say it depends how his body reacts and how the next forty-eight hours go."

Kayode clears his throat. "When he wakes up, tell him…tell him I still miss him sometimes."

"What?" I knew Kayode always had a crush on Roberto, but I never knew they may have had something.

"I will."

"Tell him I'm happy too and that he was right."

"I will, I promise." She steps to the side of me to hug Kayode, as if he's the one needing comforting. Not her.

"I think I need to go to the night nurse. I'll be back in the morning," Kayode says after kissing her on the cheek and giving me a long look. A long look I'm not sure how to interpret.

When he closes the door behind him, Em takes a deep breath and falls down on the chair by our messy desk. She usually straightens it up whenever she's close by, kind of a tick of hers. But today, she looks at it without doing anything, without any comments. She glances up and even though there are no tears in her

eyes, I feel her pain radiating through. "My father is my real father." She pauses. "And I feel like I'm in a fucking *Star Wars* movie or something. I feel like a voiceover is going to come behind me to explain what this all means. Because I can't. I don't know what it means. I don't know what to do or what to say. And it's all bullshit." Her voice rises with each word. She stands up and paces around the small room, kicking a shirt that was on the floor to the other side. "I don't know what to do. Nonna would know. Why didn't he say anything?"

"Wait…wait. Your father is…" I shake my head and enounce the words slowly. "He's your real dad?"

"Yep. That's him. My dad."

"So…he…" I'm having trouble forming coherent thoughts. "He's really your father?"

"The one and only. Why didn't he tell me before? Didn't he see it was breaking me to not know? Why did he come up with all that shit?"

"Maybe he was scared."

"Maybe he's an asshole."

"I don't know how to defend your dad, but I'm pretty sure he just got caught in all his lies, didn't know how to make everything better."

"How about telling the truth? How about trying to stop protecting himself?"

"I'm sure he wanted to." And I'm not sure why I am indeed defending him. I'm not sure why…except that I don't think Em can handle being madder at her dad than she is now.

And then she stops pacing, she stares down at her shoes. "I have a sister." This time there are tears in her voice. "And I don't even know her name. I don't even know why he didn't adopt her. Why didn't I ask my stupid father these things? God. I just… I just needed to leave, you know? I wasn't thinking… I wasn't thinking straight." Her shoulders shake and she steps forward, her hair in her face and her lips trembling. She wraps her arms around me, buries her head into my chest, holds on to me like I'm the only one who can keep her ashore.

Between her sobs, she repeats her father's exact words. She tells me how she's afraid to tell Rob when he wakes up, how she's afraid it's going to hamper his recovery.

"I want to meet her," she whispers. "We're twins. We have to look alike. But are we exactly the same? And why didn't I have this extra sense people always talk about? I didn't feel her. I didn't know."

"Maybe you did."

"What?"

"Remember, two years ago I think it was, you hurt your foot, or at least you thought it was hurting, but nothing showed up on the X-ray."

"Yes, I remember Rob telling me I was only trying to get attention, but he still looked worried."

"Maybe there was a link."

She stares at me and purses her lips. "Well, not exactly. I may have been trying to get your attention on that one."

"You did?"

"Of course, you were helping me walk, which means you were getting close to me, and I didn't want

to stop so even if it didn't hurt anymore, I may have still made it seem like it did."

"I know that," I tell her and her eyes widen. She's even blushing a little. And I'm tempted to kiss her, to make her forget everything, but instead I simply pull her to sit down next to me. Our bodies are aligned and it's like we'll be melting into one but without kissing, without touching. I take a deep breath to make sure my brain stays on course and doesn't follow all those other images I have in my mind: Em's skin, my mouth on her skin, her naked skin.

I clear my throat. "Anyways, even if you faked it for a few days, it was real at the beginning. And as for your dad, I'm not sure what happened. I'm not sure how your dad kept hiding everything, but I did too. I didn't tell you about dating those other girls so I could stay in the School, so my father continued to foot the bill."

"It's not the same."

"I'm not sure." And I'm really am not sure. Is one lie not as bad as the other? What scale does one use to decide that? Who decides it?

She shakes her head. "Your dad was only trying to protect you, though. He didn't do it right, but he was only trying to protect you. My father cheated on my mom, cheated on all of us, he cheated your dad on the business. He's a fraud on everything. And I don't know why."

"Maybe he was only trying to be someone he wasn't."

"Maybe. But I'm not sure how anything is going to work from now on. I'm not even sure Mom will ever speak to him again. She told me everything was going to be okay. But I can't even imagine how she must feel."

I caress her hair. It's so soft and she nuzzles closer to me. Her breath is on my neck, making me warm…everywhere.

"You will figure it out. I trust your mom, she'll make sure you do figure it out."

She wiggles so that her face is closer to mine. She softly kisses my cheek, and then my lips. "Thank you. For being there."

"I wouldn't be anywhere else."

CHAPTER 39 - EM

WAKING UP IN Nick's arms is warm and comforting. He stirs in his sleep and opens his eyes. He smiles and tightens his embrace, kissing my neck first tentatively, and then with so much passion that I'm no longer warm, I'm on fire.

"I could get used to that," he whispers, and I'm pretty sure my voice has disappeared right along with my common sense. I'm still sad and scared but with Nick, I feel like it's going to be okay. I feel like he gives me the strength I didn't know I had. And allows me to be weak when I need to be.

His breathing accelerates and his eyes search mine. I try to smile at him, but his hands no longer caress my back, they stop and he exhales loudly. "Good morning," he says and kisses me gently.

"Why did you stop?"

"Because I don't want to see sadness in your eyes when we make love for the first time."

I giggle. I can't help it. "Did you say 'make love'?"

"I was thinking about saying 'doing it,' but it didn't feel right. Not with you." He chuckles. "It may have sounded like a line from a movie, but I meant it."

"I know you did." I kiss him, my heart heavy and light, full of love and full of sadness. My heart beating a thousand beats per second, like right before going on stage, right before leaping in the air, right before our first kiss. "I love you," I whisper and this time when he kisses me, he takes his time.

"I love you too," he says and his lips trail down my neck. He looks into my eyes again and I try to will all of the sadness away because the way he makes me feel has nothing to do with my tears.

His hands explore under my shirt, they're warm against my skin.

The door opens wide. "I knew I should have knocked." Kayode laughs. "I'm not looking, I promise, but we do have class in forty minutes and I need to at least change." He hides his eyes behind his hand.

I kiss Nick on the cheek and sit up, almost hitting my head on the bunk bed. "I want to go back to the hospital," I say.

"Let me ask my dad to call the doctor."

"Wow, you guys know how to cut sexy times short." He winks. "You do look better, Em. Even though hickies are so not in anymore."

I touch my neck, my mouth half open. Remembering the feel of Nick's lips on my skin. Remembering the feel of Nick's hands on my skin. Remembering the feel of his body against mine.

My entire face feels way too hot.

ALWAYS SECOND BEST

Kayode chuckles. "That hicky was all worth it though, based on Em's face." He grabs some clothes inside the closet, throws them on his bed.

Nick squeezes my shoulder and whispers, "It definitely was worth it."

And my face feels flushed.

Nick kisses my cheek and gets up to grab his phone. He dials a number and within two seconds, we can faintly hear his father's voice on the other end. He asks him if he could get an update for us, or if he heard anything. And then he does something he hasn't done in forever when talking to his father, and I can't help but wonder if I'll ever be at this stage with my dad: he smiles and says, "Thank you. Thank you so much." He adds, "Dad."

And that one word means so much to both of them

And that one word kills me on the inside.

CHAPTER 40 – NICK

DAD AGREED THAT I could skip school this weekend—despite the rehearsals. I didn't really ask him, but it was still nice to have his green light. I went back to the hospital with Em, but she still couldn't see Rob, and her parents were nowhere to be seen. Maybe they were talking, maybe they were fighting. Em doesn't need that extra stress.

"Are you sure you want to stay here alone?" I ask her for the tenth time.

"I think you need to talk with your dad. It's the moment. Everything is coming out—it's time for you to really face him," she says. "And I want to be there for Rob when he wakes up, and I want to be there for Mom when she gets here. She must be getting coffee."

As if on cue, Em's mother enters the waiting area. She's not holding coffee but a bottle of water and some snacks, including Twizzlers. Em's favorite candy. "Good morning," she says and hands Em a Twizzler. Em takes it and she rushes to her mom. Her

mom opens her arms and hugs her. "I told you it's going to be fine, honey. It's going to be fine."

"I'm so sorry," Em says and her tone breaks me. She sounds like she believes she's responsible for what happened, and she's not responsible for any of those decisions. She didn't make them.

Her mom kisses the top of her head. "You have nothing to be sorry about. You are not and were not responsible for any of your father's actions. We're going to figure this out. Together." She smiles at me. "I'm sorry you were brought into all of this, Nick. But thanks for being here."

"You really don't have to thank me," I reply, shifting on my feet.

"But I want to. I know you're busy and you have your rehearsals and everything else. And I know it was difficult with your parents." She pauses. "I talked to your mom last night. We both agree that none of this should affect you two." She glances from me to Em, who seems to be looking for someone. Her eyes keep on darting to the door. "She seems to be doing well. She was going to volunteer at a homeless shelter. Something about needing to give back."

"She's working on things."

Em clears her throat. "Is Dad here?"

"Your dad moved out last night." She sounds so sad. "He'll still be in your life, I promise. We're going to make this work. But we also need to work on things, as a couple. And I'm not sure I'll be able to forgive him."

"Because of me?" she asks.

"Because of what he did. Not because of you. Never because of you, I promise."

I almost feel like an intruder. I shift on my feet, clear my throat, rub the back of my neck. "I'm going to go see my father at home, and then I'll be back."

Em lets go of her mother's hand and throws her arms around me. I hold on to her for a few seconds. "Call me if you need anything, promise?"

"Promise," she replies and I kiss her cheek.

I hope she knows that I'm strong enough to help her, that she's not alone.

CHAPTER 41 – EM

I LOOK AT MOM, at the dark circles under her eyes and search for the right words but there are none. "What's going on with Dad?"

Mom caresses my hair. "Honey, it's complicated." She sighs. "I don't think I'll be able to forgive your father enough to let him in my life again."

"That's because of me, right?"

"No. It's not. He cheated on me, he lied to me. He lied to you. He also lied for the past year, telling me he was going to work while he quit his job as financial advisor in that small firm. I'm not even sure what he's been doing. He never tells me the truth; it's little lies and big lies. Your father has issues…and I need to protect myself."

She looks so sad and yet so determined.

"And I need to protect you and Rob, and your grandmother's restaurant."

"What?"

"Your grandmother gave me her restaurant. It almost seems like she knew more about her son than she let on."

"Are you going to keep it?"

"I want to. And I want you to think about something."

"What?"

"Think about what you want. Think about what makes you happy. Because, honey, I've learned that no relationships will fulfill you completely. You need to make sure you do something for you."

"I am. I am dancing."

"But, is that what you really want? The last time I saw you happy. Really happy. It was when you were in the kitchen with Nonna. Think about it."

She gives me a kiss on the cheek and, with her head high, she leaves the hospital.

CHAPTER 42 - NICK

IT DOESN'T TAKE me long to get home. Mom is back from her volunteering. She and Dad are in the living room, talking. I can hear both their voices, but then I hear another one. Dino. Em's father's here too.

I stride into the living room. "Dad, can I talk to you?"

Dino stands up and he smells like alcohol and like he hasn't showered in a few days. "Have you seen her? Have you seen Em?"

"She's at the hospital with her mom."

"I screwed it all up. Everything," he says, and Mom shakes her head.

"Come on, Dino. Drink some water, eat something, and then we'll talk." She sounds soothing and like it isn't the first time she's had to say this in her life.

"Dad?" I ask.

"Let's go into the office," he says. I follow him, rehearsing what I'm going to say in my mind.

Dad sits in the chair behind his desk and he's sitting tall, like he does when he's negotiating a deal. This time I don't want to be one of his deals.

I pull the chair in front of the desk and sink into its leather cover. I run my finger on the old oak and then clear my throat. He's waiting for me to talk first, that's his strategy, but this time I'm ready. This time I'm not trying to simply butt heads with him. This time, I'm doing this for what I want.

"Why did you ask me to date those girls?"

"I didn't think it would be a problem."

"Why?"

"Because I thought I raised you to say no if you really didn't want to do it. You defied me on everything else: the school, the Morettis."

"You liked the Morettis."

"Yes, I did. And I still do."

"You knew I didn't want to date those girls. Why did you blackmail me into it?"

"First, I asked you to take them out, I never asked you to date them, date them."

"Come on, Dad." He's using his diversion technique. "I'm not yelling. I'm not arguing. I want to understand."

"I asked you to take out those girls when it became obvious Dino had issues. He has a gambling problem. I knew the adoption was going to come back and bite him in the ass. He lied to his wife, he lied to his daughter and he lied to me. Those pensioners losing their money was not my fault. That was his."

"Why not tell me?"

"Because I'm not a saint." He glances around. "Everything in here, it didn't come with me always

playing by the rules. I learned to manipulate the system." His eyes focus on me. "I learned to manipulate you."

"How about ballet?"

"I still don't think you can make a living out of it. I still don't think it's the career for you. And I still will not support you if you pursue this direction without gaining anything on your own." He sounds serious and like he's thought about this a lot.

"What if I do something else? What if I try teaching and then maybe still dance, but not in one of the biggest companies?"

"Are you asking me if I'd approve?"

"I don't know. Maybe." I'm not sure what I want to hear, what I want his answer to be.

He grabs the plaque on his desk, the one that says "Thank you to Grawski & Son for Your Donation" from Hospital North. He got it only a few weeks ago. It joins the dozens he already has for his charity donations.

"I wanted you to keep the family business alive. I still want you to. You could still change your path. Your grades aren't bad and with our family name, I could get you into a good college."

I look at him. Really look at him. The lines around his eyes, the way he joins his hands together and rests his chin on them, staring at me, staring me down. But not this time—this time I won't back away.

"I don't want that. I don't think it's fair of you to ask me something that isn't necessary. It's not like I really need to follow in your footsteps." And because I can't help it. And because this truce is still brand new. "Your footsteps aren't the greatest anyways."

He chuckles. "I was wondering if you were going to bite at all during this conversation."

"I won't date someone or take them out or however you want to call it ever again because you ask me to. Because you blackmail me. And I will go out with Em. I will fight for her. And I will fight for what I want."

"What do you want?" His voice rises and takes on this steely calmness that used to terrorize me when I was a kid and that used to annoy me until recently. But not now.

"I want to dance. I want to teach. I want to be with Em."

He expels air loudly and leans back in his chair. That's a new move. "I won't help you with the dancing part. I refuse to help you. My father didn't help me."

"And look how great that turned out," I mutter, and my father raises an eyebrow. Shit. Did I get that from him?

This time when he chuckles, it's more natural, like it escaped him. "I still won't help you out. I want you to figure out your way. Because let's face it. You also went out with those girls because you were afraid I wouldn't pay for the School. You didn't try to convince me except by showing me how good you were. You didn't try to find another way to pay for it or to get scholarships. You thought you were standing up to me, but you weren't." He puts the award he still had in his hand back behind his phone. "Today is the first day you not only stood up to me, but you actually talked to me."

ALWAYS SECOND BEST

I want to protest, I want to say he's wrong, I want to yell and storm out. But, he's not entirely wrong. His methods suck. Majorly suck. But I never really tried to find another way to get what I wanted until now.

His smile widens. "Dr. Grahams would be so proud of us."

This time, I smile too—it's not an "I forgive you" smile, it's more a "let's try to figure this out" smile.

But then his brows furrow and he tilts his chin down. "I haven't been a great father. I haven't been a great husband. Frankly, I haven't been a great human being either. But I'm trying to change and to be better. For your mom, for you and for me."

"I know. I do pay attention in counseling too." I pause. "How about Em's father?"

"Dino and I go way back. Before you kids, before our marriages, before we made it big. I won't give up on him. I won't let him near you and I still think he's a bad influence and that he needs to get his act together, but I won't give up on him."

That explains why Dino always rushed to my father despite the fact they had a fallout. That explains why my father was paying for Em's school. That explains why sometimes I can look at my father and be proud.

"Let's go back to see your mom, before she thinks we killed one another." He tilts his chin to the portrait of his father on the wall. "My father died a sad man, alone. I don't want to be like him. And I don't want you to be like him."

I stare at Grandfather's portrait. At the way his lips are pursed, at the way his eyes are staring straight ahead without any passion in them, at the way he looks like the world owes him and not like he owns the world.

And for the third time in a short week, I agree with my father.

CHAPTER 43 – EM

DAD'S ON ONE SIDE of the waiting room. Mom and I are on the other. The smell of the hospital is starting to be more soothing than scary. Roberto's safe. He's out of the woods and they managed to save his kidneys. He will need to follow a strict regimen and he's going to stay in the hospital for at least two more weeks, but he's no longer in danger.

"Mrs. and Mr. Moretti, Roberto is ready to take visitors. Only five minutes though."

We all jump off our seats and follow the nurse. She's giving us instructions and information. Mom and Dad are walking close to one another. Mom told me to not say anything to Roberto yet. To wait until he was out of the hospital. To not put his recovery at risk.

I agree, but I also think they don't want to say anything because they have no clue how. They don't know what to do.

My parents brush against one another on their way into the room, and they stare at each other for

three seconds before going their separate ways. There was so much in those three seconds: hurt, betrayal, and still…a bit of tenderness. Which is so weird. Because I know Mom threw up three times last night and cried until she had no tears left. "Hi," Roberto says. And I do a double take. He looks so small in his hospital gown, in the hospital bed, with tubes going out of his nose and out of his arm. He looks so pale and so broken and it hits me again that we almost lost him. We almost lost him.

Note to self: never take anyone for granted.
Note to self: do not cry.
Correction: do not cry too much.

"You look like you've seen a ghost," Roberto says and his voice croaks, but he's smiling. "The nurses told me the hospital gown looks good on me. What do you think?"

"You don't look too bad." I smooth the bedsheet. "Don't scare me like that ever again."

"I won't."

Mom and Dad have tears in their eyes. Dad pushes a strand of hair away from Rob's face. "You're going to need to take it easy."

"I will. I promise. You guys need to stop looking so sad. I'm here. I'm not going anywhere."

He closes his eyes for a second. "I'm still tired though. It's like I'm never getting enough sleep."

"Maybe you should rest," Mom says. "But we're right there. The doctor agreed I could stay in the room." She caresses his forehead.

"And I'll come back later today." Dad kisses Roberto's cheek.

"Me too." I squeeze his hand.

ALWAYS SECOND BEST

That's when Roberto would usually make a joke, where he would try to defuse the situation, but he closes his eyes again. "Love you," he whispers.

Dad walks past me without even acknowledging my presence. He hasn't talked to me. But I didn't expect him to. I have no idea where he's staying, what he's doing. I need to talk to him. I need to know. "Dad." My hand touches his arm. Briefly. "Can we talk?"

He turns to me. "What's there to say?"

"I want to know what happened. I need to know what happened. You can't drop something like this and expect me to not ask any questions.

"I didn't want it to come out like this. I really thought I'd take this secret with me to the grave." He gestures for me to follow him to the hospital's cafeteria.

He's no longer walking with his head high. He's no longer walking like he owns the world. He's no longer walking like my father.

The cafeteria is almost empty, and we find a somewhat discreet spot by the window overlooking the parking lot.

"I really wish everything would be different."

"That's not what I'm asking. I want to know what happened. I want to know about my sister. I want to know why you didn't even want her."

"I didn't know you had a sister until a few years ago. Claire and I…Claire and I were not a one-night mistake, we had a relationship. Your mom and I

hit a difficult time when we were trying to have a baby, and I was stupid, and Claire was there and she understood me."

"You lied to Mom again. I can't believe you lied again. You told us it was a one-time thing."

"I've talked to your mom. She knows. Claire found out she was pregnant after we broke it off. And she thought that we would get back together. I didn't want to. I didn't want to lose your mom, and Claire lost it."

"What do you mean?"

"She was full of rage. Full of anger. She said she was going to tell everyone about us, that she was going to tell your mom. I paid for her silence."

"Money changed her mind?"

"I was important back then. I was convincing. I was her boss. And I promised her she would be destroyed if she tried anything against me. That I would destroy her."

I stare at him. I can't reconcile the image of my father—of the man who played with us, cuddled with us, disguised himself as Santa Claus every year—with the man sitting across from me.

He shakes his head. "She destroyed me at the end. We worked side by side for almost eight years after our affair."

"Eight years?" My eyes widen—this seems like such a long time for people to work together after everything that happened.

"Yes. She needed the job, I needed to keep face. This was torture. Then, she quit. Four years ago, she called me up. Apparently she had been working on herself. Her husband wanted her to come clean, she

said." His hands shake a little. "She told me that you had a twin sister, that she kept her away from me, because she wanted to punish me and to keep a part of me. She asked if I wanted to meet her. If I wanted to know her name. If I wanted to know anything." He licks his lips and avoids my gaze.

A pit forms in my stomach the size of the crater Roberto built for a science fair when he was seven. "What did you say? What's her name?"

"I said I didn't want to know. I said this part of my life was over. I said she should never call me again." His voice trembles. "I got scared."

"You got scared!" I stand up so fast the chair tumbles down. I pick it up and face him. He's still sitting, not moving, still not looking at me. "She's my sister. She's your daughter. You lied to us for so many years."

"I thought I could put it all behind me. I love your mom. I love her so much. And I love you guys too. You have to see this. I was only trying to do what was best. And I lost everything. My family, my job, my mother."

Tears blur my vision and I blink my eyes rapidly. "I don't know what to say. Why didn't you come clean last summer? Why? You saw how devastated I was and you said nothing."

"I didn't know how. I lied for so many years, I almost believed my truth." He pauses. "You've got to help me. Talk to your mom. Tell her to give me another chance."

I freeze. "I can't be in the middle. I can't even look at you and realize that you're my father. All those years where I wondered who my father may be, you were right there."

"I have to go." He stands up. His hands shake even more now. "You know the truth. And see? It killed everything." He strides away from me. "It killed everything," he says louder, and he sounds like a madman.

He doesn't sound like my father.

It takes me about fifteen minutes to gather the strength to leave the cafeteria. I hesitate between sadness and fury, between tears and the desire to scream my lungs out.

I head out. A girl in a tutu hurries ahead of me. This black straight hair, the oversized bag with the logo of the School of Performing Arts…what's Jen doing here?

"Jen!" I call her name and she turns around. She's got the saddest smile on. "What are you doing here?"

She clears her throat, shifts on her feet—totally unlike her usual behavior. "Nothing."

"You happened to come to the hospital in your tutu."

"My sister is in this hospital. And she's five. And she's very sick. And once a week, I come and dance for the kids here."

She looks on the verge of tears—gone is the fierce attitude, the big mouth, the I-know-everything smile.

"I'm sorry. I didn't know."

"I haven't told anyone." She shrugs. "I have to maintain my image." She laughs bitterly. "And I don't want to talk about it, because every single time I think

about it, I want to cry and I want to scream and I want to hide away. Dancing is the only thing that really helps me deal with all of this."

"Oh."

She shakes her head. "Yes, oh. I know I'm a bitch sometimes. And there are times I know I shouldn't be and wish I could apologize but other times, I think being a bitch isn't such a bad thing. Being a bitch simply means I tell the truth to those who don't want to hear it." She pauses. "Like now, I'm about to be a bitch to you."

"Okay."

She exhales loudly. "You need to get your head out of your ass and realize what it is you want to do. Because some people don't even have the choice to be anybody. My sister is going to die. And you're wasting your chance because you think you need to make everyone else happy but yourself. And that's pissing me off." She's crying now and I pull her toward me. She sniffles. "You're a hugger. Of course you are." And she cries in my arms.

And I know she's right.

CHAPTER 44 - NICK

THE NEXT DAY at school, I double my efforts, I stay in the moment, I focus. Even if my mind drifts to a picture of Em crying, to the way Rob looked before the ambulance took him away.

I force myself to keep on going.

"Svetlana?" I call at the end of the last class. She's taking notes in her notebook, and bites the pen when I approach.

"Everything okay?" She looks more tired than I've ever seen her.

"Fine. I was wondering if there was a program for student teachers or if the school takes volunteers. I'd like to take a year off after I graduate."

"A year off? But with the showcase, you could have the world of ballet at your feet." She bites her pen again and then puts it on the chair behind her. "It's a bad habit I have, I'm sorry. I used to bite my nails, but I got this very bad tasting nail polish and I stopped."

She shakes her head. "Anyways. Why would you want to take a year off?"

"I love dancing."

"I know you do. You're amazing. You're one of the most talented dancers we've had in years, and I don't say this lightly."

"Thank you," I reply and rub the back of my neck. "I do love dancing, but I'm not sure I want to be in a ballet company and dance other people's choreographies and travel or forget everything else that's not dancing."

"Nobody says you have to do that."

"I just…I've worked so hard at proving to my father that I wanted to be a dancer, that I was good enough to be a dancer, that I forgot why I was doing it in the first place. I feel like I need to find my way again to what I want."

"So you'd like to volunteer?"

"I don't know if…I'd like to have the possibility to live in the dorms and to help you teach."

"Me?" She scratches her skin and then bites her nail. "I forgot about that stupid nail polish." She grimaces. "Let me talk to the school director and I'll get back to you." She pauses. "But Nick. I think it's very mature of you to think this through and to not jump headfirst. Your parents must be proud."

"Maybe. I guess we'll see," I reply. "Do you mind if I stay a bit longer to rehearse?"

"Of course you can."

And this time when I dance, when I repeat the same movement a thousand times, even if it's killing me, I'm also enjoying every second.

Before going to see Rob, the last time I went to the hospital was when my grandfather passed away. I still remember him taking his last breath. I was sixteen and I didn't want to be there. The Clorox sickness smell churned my stomach and the way my grandfather looked, small and gray, haunted me for weeks after. I wasn't close to my grandfather, he was my dad's father and clearly he didn't think my father was good enough. That hospital visit was the one day I saw my dad squirm on his seat and try too hard.

I pass the nurses' stations and give them my ID. I'm eighteen so I'm allowed to visit alone. I turn into the second right and Rob's door is open. He's laughing. I never thought hearing him laugh would make me smile like that.

He's on the phone and I sit on the chair by his bed. "You told her what?" he asks and laughs again. "You're going to get in so much trouble!" He waves at me. "Giovanni, I'll talk to you later." He nods and whispers something and chuckles and whispers something else that sounds a lot like "I love you" in Italian.

Then he turns to me. "I heard you saved my life. I think it's all those video games we played, you had the right reactions."

"Must be it. You, on the other hand, are supposed to be a prodigy. Aren't you supposed to know when you should stop dicking around and see a doctor?"

"Dicking around? In what sense? Because I am monogamous." He pauses. "And you are too. Right? I

mean you are seeing my sister." We both stare at each other and I'm not sure who laughs first, but soon enough a nurse pops in the room.

"You both need to be a bit quieter. Some patients are trying to rest."

"Sorry," I say and Roberto closes his eyes. Maybe laughing like that tired him. Maybe he's not feeling well.

He opens an eye again. "Giovanni had been worried sick. He sent several messages to me after he couldn't contact me, and then to Emilia."

"She did write to him, right?"

"She did. But it was after twenty-four hours so he was freaking out." He pauses. "I really really like this guy."

"I know."

"But what if he never comes out to his family? Why does it have to be so hard?"

"I have no clue." Rob told me he was gay in middle school. Right after he defended me against bullies who beat the shit out of me because I was a dancer and thus in their words "had to be a pussy." He told his parents not long after, and it didn't seem to change anything for them. They only want him to be happy.

Rob clears his throat. "My Nonna really loved him too. I miss her. Thanks for coming to the funeral."

"You already thanked me, and you really don't need to."

"Can you thank your father though? He hasn't come to see me and I know he did a lot for me."

"I will." We both turn to the TV at the same time—there's a documentary about Comic-Con. We look at each other, and then turn it up.

Sometimes, everything seems so easy…But it's not easy.

Rob still looks sick and he's got a long way ahead of him and he still doesn't know about Em and his dad, but it's not my place to tell him.

CHAPTER 45 – EM

ON SATURDAY, THE wind isn't as strong anymore and the sun peeks through the clouds. I check my phone before heading out, but Natalya still hasn't texted me back. I have to ask her mom for the center address, to go see her. Sending flowers and a card isn't enough. And I understand she needs time, but maybe she also needs to know that we're there for her.

I pick up the small basil plant Nonna had standing on one of the restaurant's windows and push the door closed with my hip.

Mr. Edwards doesn't live far away, so I'm on his front steps within less than ten minutes. I put the basil between my arm and my waist and ring the doorbell.

Loud barking comes from behind the door. "Friday, come on!" And then there's some shuffling. "I'm coming!" He opens the door and his entire face lights up. "Emilia, what a pleasure to see you here!"

"I'm sorry, I don't want to intrude. I tried calling you."

"I've been busy with this monster over there." He points to the yellow lab wagging his tail behind a gate. "I adopted him last week. I thought…" His smile dims and his shoulders slump. "I thought it would do me some good to take care of a dog. I can still walk. He's old like me. The rescue said his age was the reason no one wanted him. I understand that completely." He chuckles and gestures for me to come in. "Don't stay outside."

"I have something for you." I hand him the basil. "Basil was Nonna's favorite herb and she loved that one, she said she planted it when you two met, and I thought…I thought maybe you'd like to have it."

He brings his hand to his heart. "That's very kind." The dog barks again so he raises his voice. "So very kind." He takes the basil plant from my arms and smells it for several seconds. "Your Nonna is…." He clears his throat. "She was a wonderful woman."

I shift on my feet. "She really cared about you." I imagine Nonna giving me a small nudge and I continue, "We all do. Mom and I would love to have you over for dinner next week."

"I'd love that. Do you want something to drink?"

"Yes, please."

"I can make us some tea. Friday will keep us company. He's a good dog. A barker but a good dog."

"I'd love some tea." And I follow him into his small living room. It's full of paintings and photographs. Friday licks my hand as he walks past me and plops himself on the dark red rug underneath the

table. "Did you take those pictures?" I point to the Eiffel Tower.

"I did. After the war. I don't want to bore you."

"You wouldn't. Tell me about it."

And there's something in his eyes that softens. "Your grandmother was right. You're a very special young lady, Emilia."

My throat dries up at his words. Emotions roll over me and I don't know what to do with them. So I give him a quick hug before sitting down at the table. "What type of tea do you have?"

He chuckles. "Let me see. I'll be right there." The dog follows him to the kitchen.

Each photograph on his wall captures some feeling—it's almost like dancing. And then, on the left, right by a lamp, there's one of Nonna. She's laughing. I stand up and slowly approach it like the photograph is going to come alive or Nonna is going to talk me.

She doesn't, but the photograph captured her spirit. She's in the kitchen of the restaurant and she's turning around, looking right at the camera.

Friday the Dog walks up to me and licks my hand again. It's like he feels that I need it. Mr. Edwards is right behind him. "I'll make you a copy of it if you'd like." He sets tea boxes on the table. "She was so beautiful."

"She really was. Inside and out." I put the frame back next to the lamp. "But she hated her picture being taken. So I'm sure there's a story behind it too." I sit back at the table and smile.

Something I've learned this past year, something I've learned from being loved by a mother who chose me and by a family who didn't even know I was theirs, is that people can become family. And Mr. Edwards definitely is a part of ours. He shouldn't be alone.

After my visit to Mr. Edwards, the rest of the week sticks to a routine. After school, I visit Roberto at the hospital. Sometimes, Nick comes with me. Sometimes, Mom's there. Sometimes, Dad is.

Today, we are all in the small room—minus Nick, and the atmosphere is stuffy. And heavy. And plain wrong.

"Okay, what's going on?"

"What do you mean?" Mom asks, looking up from the novel she always brings with her at the hospital. My guess is that it's one more way to avoid Dad.

"I may have been operated on but I'm not stupid."

"We'll talk once you're out of the hospital."

"What did Dad do?" he asks again, staring at me as if he knows I might be the only one to tell him the truth.

Dad stands up. "I'm sorry, son. About everything."

"We agreed we would wait," Mom hisses.

"Clearly, this is not working, Amanda. Clearly, nothing is working." His voice rises and his shoulders shake. He inhales and exhales deeply. "I'm sorry." He turns to me. "I love you, Emilia. You know that."

And despite everything that's happened, I do know that. Despite him being a jerk in the past year, and lying to me for seventeen years, I know he does love me.

"Will someone please tell me what's going on?" Roberto's voice is stronger than last week. "I swear if you don't tell me, I'm going to scream."

"How very nine-year-old of you," I tell him, remembering that's what he used to do when he didn't get his way.

"Ha-ha. Don't try to change the subject. Mom and Dad are monosyllabic with one another. There's always five feet between them. And you never look at Dad, while he's trying to engage you in a conversation. So, yep, I'm sensing something is majorly wrong." He's out of breath at the end of his little speech. But he adds, "Emilia, why don't you tell me?"

"I don't think…" I start but he shuts me up with a glare.

"I'm currently at the hospital, restrained, and receiving medical care. Do you guys really think that waiting to tell me whatever it is until I'm out and about is the best policy?" He shakes his head. "My guess is that Dad screwed up majorly. Which means it's about Em's adoption."

"He's my father," I blurt out, and Mom buries her head in her hands. While Dad simply stands there, gauging Rob, his reaction, gauging me.

"Fuck," Rob says. "Wait, what?"

Dad explains the short version of what happened and Rob's face hardens. "Get out. Get out now."

"Let me explain," Dad says, but Roberto's face contorts with pain and Dad winces as if he felt the pain too. "I'm so sorry," he says before heading out. And I think he's crying. And that still kills me.

"I can't believe it," Roberto says. "I can't believe it."

"You're not the only one." I try to chuckle but that falls flat. Roberto pats the spot on the bed close to him and I get up to lie beside him. Mom stands up and kisses both of us.

"I love you both," she says. "I love you both the same."

Roberto stares at the ceiling but then turns to me. "You've always been my sister, so that doesn't change. The only difference if that if you ever need a kidney, I'll definitely volunteer."

I hug him so hard the machines start beeping.

CHAPTER 46 – NICK

REHERSALS WENT better than yesterday. Yesterday, there was screaming and almost tears. Today, it's all smiles and applause. We did manage to bring the dance to the next level. And it seems everyone noticed it, because the entire crew was more relaxed. Emilia came to the rehearsals, but it was clear her heart wasn't in it. She's talking to Jen right now, who keeps on nodding and smiling and nodding and smiling, and seeing both of them friendly with one another is still weird.

If they hug, I'm going to call bullshit. Jen is not a hugging person. Emilia is, though, and she could convert her.

"Who knew Jen could actually be nice?" Kayode sneaks behind me and I jump.

"I knew she was nice," I reply.

"Of course you did. Up close and personal." Kayode laughs and then wraps an arm around my shoulders. "Just kidding. Well, kidding a little.

Because you did go out with Jen and you broke her heart and she kind of went psycho a bit. But it's all good now."

"Why do I have the feeling that you know everything there is to know?"

"Because I always know everything." He smiles. "Jen!" he calls and Jen turns to him. She frowns for only a split second.

"What?"

"Are you going to the recital tonight at the Met?"

"I am. Mom got me tickets. I have a feeling you want to come with me."

"That'd be great. Thanks for the invite," Kayode replies, and Jen says bye to Emilia before joining Kayode. Together, they leave the rehearsal room, leaving Em and me alone.

She stretches one more time and then turns to me. "I am going to call Claire Carter. I want to meet my sister. And honestly, I am not happy dancing anymore. I see you and I see Jen and you both suffer with a smile. I want to yell and scream and tell everyone to put Madonna on."

"I told you we should have a showcase with the eighties music your mom likes." I approach her and we both sit on the wooden floor. Our bodies are aligned with one another and I take her hand in mine, watching how small hers look compared to mine, watching how the bracelet I got her is still on her wrist, and she leans her head on my shoulder. I breathe in. I wouldn't be anywhere else but here. With her.

"Do you think it's a phase?" I ask.

"Us?"

"No, not us. I don't think we're a phase. I think we're here to stay. I'm talking about dancing. Is it something that might pass, where you're just too stressed about your mom and your brother and your dad and everything else?"

"I don't think so. I haven't felt it in a long time now. I wanted to prove something. I wanted to be first, but not having the lead in the showcase might be the best thing that's ever happened to me." She nudges me. "Well, except you, of course. You're pretty amazing."

I chuckle. "Oh, I know that. Amazing Nick. That's my superhero nickname." I kiss the top of her head.

She snuggles closer to me. "Dad hasn't been home. And he hasn't called me or anything, but I don't know."

"I can ask my father to call him if you want."

She shifts a bit to look at me. "Please."

"Of course." I bend down to give her a kiss— it's not a lingering one or a passionate one, it's one we're learning, it's the anytime-kiss. "But you still haven't told me. What are you going to do if you're not dancing?"

"My grades aren't bad. I was looking online at culinary schools last night. I thought…maybe. Maybe I could try it out and see if I like it."

"Culinary school." my lips stretch into an encouraging smile, into an I-believe-in-you smile. "I think you can do it."

"I think so too. And I loved spending time with Nonna in the restaurant. How about you? The last time we talked about the future and career and what comes

after graduation, you were more set on finding the best ballet company for you." She stares straight ahead and her body stiffens against mine.

"I've been thinking…I've asked Svetlana if I could maybe stay here one more year. As a volunteer. To teach. To take one year off. To think. I don't want to become a lawyer or join Dad in Grawski & Son, and I want to dance. And have a career out of it, but my mind is racing with ideas…with possibilities, and I'd like to take a year to think about it."

Her body relaxes again. "That means amazing Nick is sticking around."

"Sticking around, and even if I end up choosing to go to a ballet company, I'll still be amazing Nick."

She nods, and I hope she understood what I meant. So to make sure, I add, "I love you." And I never thought my heart could feel so full.

We head to our spot in Central Park. More and more people are hanging out and there's a change in the air. Like the world is ready to awaken again.

And I'm clearly spending too much time playing Prince Charming—I'm starting to talk like him.

Em clutches Claire's letter in her hand. "If she wrote down her number, that means I can call her, right?"

"I'm pretty sure that's what it means. You can do this. You know the truth now. The only thing left to do is for you to meet your sister."

"What if she hates me?"

"What if she doesn't?"

"Hmm. What am I going to tell her?" she asks and stares at the phone.

"You managed to find a common ground with Jen. Jen who you used to hate, so I'm pretty sure you'll do great with your own sister."

"Do you think she looks like me?"

"I don't know. Probably. You're twin sisters after all," I reply and then touch her hip. "Come on. You want to call. You can do it."

She takes a deep breath and dials the number.

CHAPTER 47 - EM

THE PHONE RINGS ONCE, twice. I switch hands to wipe my other one, which has become way too sweaty.

"Hello." Claire's voice is confident.

"Hi, this is Emilia. You left me your number. So I thought maybe it was okay for me to call." And I blabber and I wipe my hand again, balancing the phone between my chin and my shoulder. Nick gently rubs the back of my neck and it's soothing and he whispers. "You're fine."

"I was waiting for your call," she replies. "I'm sure you have a lot of questions. And I'm sure calling hasn't been easy. Your father told me he explained to you that you have a twin sister."

I stop breathing. "You still talk to my father?" That's not what he said. But I wouldn't be surprised if he lied again.

"No. Not really. I worked with him for almost eight years after giving birth to you and your sister." She exhales loudly as if remembering that time of her life is almost too painful. "Eight years. It seemed like it was eight hundred years at the time. Eight years of lying to him, hating him, loathing him. When I quit, I cut all contact with him, until my husband convinced me to finally come clean. I've talked to him twice since I quit. Once, when I told him about your twin sister, and the second time when your brother was at the hospital. After he refused to see me, after he threatened to bring me down, I thought it best to cut all contact."

"You did keep a baby though. His baby too. My sister."

"When I entered the maternity ward, I told myself I would tell him. I would give away both of you. At the beginning, I thought it was a way to get back at him. A way to have some leverage."

"Leverage?" My voice is way too high. I take a deep breath. "What are you talking about? You can't force someone into being in a relationship with you!"

"But that's what I thought at the time. I thought once he saw me with your sister, he'd know that we all belonged together, that we were a family." Her laugh is harsh and chills dance up and down my spine. "I was stupid. I was clearly having issues. My past isn't the best. That's not an excuse, but I wanted to hold on to your dad."

"Oookay," I say slowly. Not sure why she wanted to hold on to him so badly: he cheated on Mom with her, he threatened her, he treated her like total and utter shit when she got pregnant.

"But then, during my pregnancy, he only called to talk about my appointments, he asked to see the video of you and I gave him one of my friends' so he didn't see there were two of you. He didn't care about me. He only cared about his baby. I thought then he could have both of you. But…" She clears her throat. "But, when you and Hannah were born…"

"Hannah? Is that my sister's name?"

"Yes, Hannah. It was my mother's name."

Hannah. I whisper her name. Hannah. Emilia and Hannah.

"I was saying, when you and Hannah were born. I held her in my arms. They brought her to me first. She was screaming and she was so perfect. And she was cuddling to me and looking at me as if she knew me." Her voice cracks. "I told the doctors I didn't want to hold you. Because I knew if I held you, I wouldn't be able to let you go."

Tears spring to my eyes and Nick pulls me to him. "Why didn't you try to see me? Why didn't you try to contact me? Why did you keep her away from me too?"

"I did. I went to almost every recital. I stood in the back and always left before the end."

My throat is dry. She came to see me. She was there. Maybe, she did care. I don't understand.

She breaks the silence, as if she knows I need time to process what she just said. "I tried to gather the courage to tell your father about your sister so many times. So many times. When he broke up with me, before I found out I was pregnant, he was in tears. He said he loved your mother and that he never wanted to hurt her. He didn't care about me. Not enough anyways. And it brought me back to a bad place in my life." Someone calls her again in the background. "Give me a second."

"Okay."

Nick kisses my hand. "Do you need anything?"

"A new life story."

"Many people love you. I love you." He nudges my shoulder. "I know it's hard, but you've been waiting for this truth for so long. And you have a sister."

ALWAYS SECOND BEST

"Nothing seems easy. I want to hate my father. But I can't. I want to hate Claire, but you should have heard the despair in her voice."

"Are you still there?" Claire asks, and I put my index finger to my lips.

"I'm here."

"Anyways, when I finally had the guts to tell your dad, and to tell him that Hannah has Down syndrome, his reaction was a reminder of why it was good for me to have moved on."

I frown and narrow my eyes. "What did you say?" I don't think I heard her correctly.

"Your sister has Down syndrome."

My mouth opens, then closes, then opens again. Nick must have felt me tense because he crouches in front of me. "Are you okay?"

I shake my head, unsure.

"How is that even possible?"

"It's very rare but it happens. Trust me, I Googled it many times, trying to understand." She clears her throat. "And I didn't know about it when I was pregnant. I didn't need an amniocentesis back then and my pregnancy wasn't too complicated, despite having twins. They didn't even realize Hannah had Down syndrome until several hours after I gave birth." She pauses. "When I told your dad, he wasn't happy to say the least. He said he didn't want to have anything to do with her, but it's not true. I saw him at one of her soccer games."

"He didn't tell me that."

"Your father is complicated."

"Complicated is not the word I would have used."

"Maybe not. Anyways, I gave the nurse the ballerina blanket for you. Hannah has the same one."

I struggle to swallow my saliva. It's like it's stuck in my throat and I gulp several times. "But is she okay?"

"She's happy and bright and wonderful. Everyone loves her."

"Does she know about me?"

"My husband and I told her about you when she was eight years old. She makes you a birthday card every year."

I close my eyes. "When can I see her?"

"How about this weekend? We could come to New York. Hannah loves Central Park. She has a favorite spot, it's close to the big fountain." And as she goes on to explain Hannah's favorite spot, a happy smile forms on my lips.

"That's my favorite spot too," I tell her and my hand finds Nick's. He squeezes it. "I'll see you next week. At two p.m.? "

"Okay," she replies.

And when I hang up, I throw my arms around Nick's neck and without a word, without a question, he simply holds me.

Until I'm ready to talk.

Until I'm ready to explain what happened.

Until my tears are replaced with excitement and joy. Because, next week, next week I'm meeting my sister.

The week passes. Too slow. Too fast. Another week full of ups and downs and mainly ups. Because

ALWAYS SECOND BEST

Roberto's doing better. Because Mom's fighting for what she wants. Because I'm finally realizing who I am and what I need to do to be first.

Being first doesn't always mean the first place on the podium. Being first should be about learning what it is that makes you happy and pursuing that dream and not giving up and staying true to yourself. Being first should be about the journey.

And I'm learning as much as I can about Down syndrome. I watch videos and I try to educate myself. And I cry. A lot. But not all of them are sad tears.

My hand clutches Nick's.

My nails are digging into his skin, but I'm so nervous I can't help it.

Mom asked me if she should come, if I need the comfort, but I could see in her eyes that it would be too difficult, too much, too painful.

And Nick simply told me he'd be there if I needed him. And oh do I need him. Claire's waiting in Central Park with my sister—Hannah. She said Hannah loves going there and that she made me something special.

In my bag, I have three things for her: a ballerina poster—one I had signed by Misty Copeland when I saw her three years ago and that I told myself I'd keep for when I have an apartment of my own— some coconut cookies I made because Claire told me that was Hannah's favorite, and a picture frame that says "sisters." I hope that we'll be able to fill it with memories of our own. I don't know how to react. I don't know what I will say.

Claire and Hannah are sitting under a tree. I recognize Claire's hair and Hannah seems to be about her height.

Nick nudges my shoulder with his. "Are you sure you want to do this?"

"I am. Claire said that Hannah was looking forward to meeting me. And Hannah is my sister, you know. Why did Dad leave her behind? Why did Claire and he agree it was the best solution for everyone? I'll never understand." I take a shaky breath. "When Claire told Hannah I was a ballerina, she said dancers are magical."

"She was right. But not because you dance ballet. You are magical."

"Three days ago, you said I was an ass for pushing you to do your homework."

"You're a magical ass. And are we really talking about your ass again?"

I slap his arm but glance at him with a smile I hope isn't too wobbly. "What do I tell her?"

"Why don't you listen first? Claire told her you were coming."

I breathe in deeply—the air is a mixture of spring and of the cakes people seem to be enjoying in the field. The slight breeze is the type you look for in the summer, and everything seems so peaceful. I'm not.

The emotions within me whirl and whirl and whirl, and there's a hurricane that doesn't know where to land except right into my heart.

"She did." We step closer to them and then I clear my throat. "Hi…" I say and I'm not sure my voice carries or is loud enough, but then Hannah turns

to me and a smile breaks on her face. I look at her and yes, I see her differences, but more than anything else, I see how she's crying and I'm not sure if her tears brought mine or the other way around, but I know I'm sobbing. Loudly.

"Emilia," she says, slowly. And then she stands up and opens her arms. And I turn to Nick, who smiles at me, squeezes my hand one last time before letting it go. I rush to my sister.

She's not responsible for anything. Like I'm not. Our parents screwed up. Majorly. But we don't have to suffer for their decisions. And as she hugs me fiercely, I certainly don't feel like a mistake. And she doesn't feel like one either.

"I made you something," she says and she touches my face. "You're so pretty."

"No. You're pretty," I reply and Claire sniffles next to me.

Hannah shuffles in her bag and hands me a bracelet with little hearts on it. "The hearts are because I love you."

She smiles again. "Do you want ice cream too?" And then she glances at Nick. "Is that your boyfriend?" She blushes and speaks slowly.

I nod and she giggles.

"I have a boyfriend too. His name is Erik. And he loves me."

"I'm sure he does."

And just like that, we sit down together and we talk.

And just like that, we get to know one another.

And just like that, I have a sister.

CHAPTER 48 - EM

ANOTHER APPLICATION SENT. Check. I've managed to get my statement right on why I want to learn how to be a chef. Or at least dip my toes in the culinary world.

"Are you going out?" Mom asks from downstairs.

"In a few minutes! I'm spending the evening at Nick's," I reply.

"I have to go to the restaurant until late. Don't wait for me."

"I won't!" I tell her. She opens the door of my room and kisses my forehead.

"You look pretty," she says, glancing down at my outfit. I did take extra care of what I was going to wear—it's not over the top, but it is one of my nicest tops, one that actually makes it look like I have boobs, and the dark-washed boyfriend jeans that I know I look good in. I feel good.

"Thanks," I reply.

ALWAYS SECOND BEST

"Don't stay up too late, and don't forget that tomorrow your father is calling you."

I sigh. "I remember." We're taking baby steps. But they're steps nonetheless. So I call them progress. I send him a confirmation email—he apparently believes I was going to cancel again. And he's not entirely wrong. I wanted to, but then he's raised me for so long, and he's raised me right until at least last year. I haven't entirely forgiven Claire or him for what they've done. Done to me. Done to Mom. Done to Hannah.

I quickly reply to Giovanni, who's trying to plan a surprise for Roberto—he'd like all of Roberto's friends, including the ones studying abroad or all the way in California, to shoot him little "feel well" messages. I'm helping as much as I can.

But I keep on looking at one card that Nonna wrote to me four years ago when I was in the Hamptons. She wrote her usual happy news about her and Poppa and the restaurant and the food we needed to try together, and then she signed by saying, "The weak can never forgive. Forgiveness is the attribute of the strong." Which I've learned since then is a quote by Gandhi. At the time I thought she was talking about Roberto and how I needed to forgive him for having beheaded one of my dolls and taken the arms out of the other for his experiment. Even as a kid, he believed in science. I reread the words and trace the letters with my fingers. Warmth spreads all over me. Maybe that was a message to me about my father. Maybe she knew. Maybe she wants me to forgive.

I shake my head. I've been watching too many Lifetime movies the past days.

I grab my coat and hurry out of the house.

I avoid a big puddle of water on the sidewalk and tilt my head to the rain. Feeling alive. Feeling like everything is possible. Feeling like I can taste my future. The future I can build for myself.

The doorman lets me in at Nick's and as soon as I step in, Nick gathers me in his arms. "Are you ready for the tournament of doom?" He laughs.

"Do you mean, are you ready for me to kick your ass?"

"Oh, Em, always talking about asses."

I nudge him and let my hand trail down his shoulder slowly. He's wearing a dark buttoned shirt and a pair of jeans and he's got a faint cologne smell and his hair is still wet and the way he smiles melts my entire body.

"Come on, let's go," he says.

"Where are your parents?"

"Gone for the weekend."

"So, it's just you and me."

"And the marathon of zombie video games," he replies and kisses my lips. "You look worried."

"Not...worried." I gulp. "Worried is not the word."

"Okay."

I follow him up the stairs, to his room. We sit on the floor and he turns on his PS4. "Are you ready?"

"I think I am," I reply, and he doesn't get what I mean. And I don't know what to do to show him. So I settle closer to him and grab one of the controllers.

Our arms touch, our knees touch and as we attack the zombies, I swear the electricity between us ripples. It grows, it magnifies, it's like being on stage, under the spotlights, but multiplied a thousand times, it's like our first kiss but multiplied a million times. I catch him looking at me and then glancing away. He's nervous, I can tell by the way he plays—not great. He's happy, I can tell by the way he smiles—it's his real smile.

A zombie attacks us and eats us. We're about to lose the game, the universe will be overflown with zombies, but we don't care. It's a moment in the air, one moment before a kiss. One moment. And when our hands brush again, he interlinks his fingers with mine. He kisses the palm of my hand and then he whispers my name and he kisses me. His lips mold into mine. And I don't want to stop.

CHAPTER 49 – NICK

I DON'T THINK I'll ever get enough of her. Of the way her lips taste, of the way her skin's so soft under my fingers, of the way she melts right into my arms.

"Em," I whisper. My voice is husky. My hands are buried into her hair, pulling her closer to me, closer, always closer.

There's a side of my brain that tells me to slow down, to breathe deeply, but her lips graze my neck and her breath is hot and my other brain is going with the program.

Somehow, we end up lying on the floor. She's on top of me and she's got to feel how this all turns me on. But instead of stopping, she slowly unbuttons my shirt. Her hands tremble.

"We don't have to," I say while my head and my entire body are screaming: *"Please, please, don't stop."*

"I know we don't have to," she says and her eyes are shining. Not with tears. With something entirely different that tightens my chest with happiness. "I know I don't want to."

"Are you sure?" My throat is dry and my hands fumble under her shirt.

"I'm sure. I want you to be my first. I want you."

And her words are as tempting and as sexy as the way she looks at me right now, licking her lower lip, unsure yet so bold. She takes off my shirt and then shrugs her off and she leans on me and feeling her skin against mine is almost too much, and I breathe in deeply.

She kisses me and I roll us over so that I'm now on top of her. My fingers graze her stomach, down, down, down. And she stiffens, so I take it more slowly.

"Do you have…you know?" she asks and then clears her throat again. "A condom. Do you have a condom?"

I nod and grab my wallet. I always have one.

"Next time, I'll plan. But I wasn't sure. And then I was sure. And then I didn't know." She blabbers and she's adorable and hot and smart and funny and she's Em. And I can't believe she's in my arms.

I go as slow as possible and her eyes widen. Her breathing accelerates and she moans my name. And I'm about to explode.

"Are you sure?" I ask again because I don't want her to regret one single second of what's about to happen.

"I'm sure," she replies. And then she moves her head up as I bend mine down and we bump into one another. And shit. But she laughs—that happy laugh of hers and I chuckle right alongside with her.

"We let the zombies eat us," she whispers.

"All worth it," I reply and she smiles.

And her hands fumble down my back and she's touching my ass and she's laughing again. "Are you laughing about my ass?" I ask and then wink. "Because I know how interested you are about asses and all."

She blushes and I kiss her lips. "You can touch me anywhere," I tell her and this time when we kiss, there's no awkwardness, no head bumping, it's hot and feverish and it's everything.

And when we're one, I keep on staring into her eyes, cradling her face with one of my hands, lifting myself up so I don't crush her and when she winces, I kiss her and when she closes her eyes and moves with me, I whisper, "I love you."

And then I forget everything that's not her.

CHAPTER 50 - EM

THE EVENING WITH NICK was…amazing. It was awkward at times when we bumped our heads, or when I didn't know where to put my hands at the beginning, or when he asked if what he was doing was okay. But once we passed that stage, it meant something. And the way he cared for me before, during and after, cuddling me and laughing with me and talking about nothing and everything, meant the world.

Now, when his arm goes around my waist, my face flushes remembering how he looks underneath, remembering what we've done and what we're planning on doing again.

"Earth to Emilia," Nick tells me, kissing my cheek. "We're going to be late for Roberto's Welcome Home party." He grins my favorite half-grin. "And I know that look. We cannot go kill zombies right now."

And I chuckle. Because that's become our code word for sex and his fingers graze my waist and I want to lean in, but instead I grab the gift we got Roberto. As a couple.

"Do you think he's going to like it?"

"He's going to throw himself at our feet."

I cross my fingers he's right. "Let's go."

The party is in Nonna's restaurant. Hannah is going to be there and it's the first time she's going to meet Roberto. Claire agreed that we could spend more time together. I'm not even sure Dad is going to show up. But I don't think he will. Especially since I told him Hannah is coming too. Once a coward, always a coward.

And clearly, I've moved past the bitter stage. Not.

I helped Mom decorate the entire place with science-related things like mad scientists paper plates, an erupting volcano, $E=MC^2$ banderoles. And Nonna's old kitchen crew helped me put together the food. Lasagna. Nonna's recipe.

My eyes prickle and I take a deep breath, remembering how Nonna always loved family parties. Mr. Edwards is there too. And I go give him a hug.

"Thank you for having me here."

Mom steps to us. "You're part of the family," she says. "You're always welcome."

And my heart bursts with pride. Mom may be going through the toughest time of her life, but she's getting the help she needs and she's true to herself.

Hannah arrives shortly after. She's alone, even though I did tell her she could bring Erik, but apparently he was working today and didn't want to take off because he works hard. That's how she explained it to me.

"Emilia!" she says and there's a beautiful smile on her face. She throws her arms around me and I hug her back. Mom clears her throat and excuses herself right after saying "hi." I'm sure it's not easy on her. But she insisted Roberto needed to meet Hannah too.

"Hi Nicholas," Hannah says, blushing a little.

Nick gives her a kiss on the cheek. "Hi, beautiful Hannah. Did you have a good week?"

"The best one. Mom and Dad took me back to Central Park and I got to draw and I am applying to jobs," she says, standing a bit taller.

"They're coming," someone yells.

There are loud voices outside. A friend from Roberto's school picked him up and Roberto complained how we've all forgotten about him already. To make up for it, we said we'd meet for dinner here. I'm sure he suspects something, but whatever.

When the door opens, we all jump up. "Surprise!"

Roberto laughs and bows down. "I knew it. You guys are the best!" He goes around, hugging people and kissing them, assuring them he's no longer contagious.

He stops in front of Hannah. His eyes slide from me to her and then he smiles. "Hi," he says.

And she hugs him too and he hugs her back and there are tears in his voice when he says, "Welcome to the family, Hannah!"

"Welcome to the family, Rob!" she replies and they both laugh.

And then I press the button and the video Giovanni prepared starts up.

Roberto is moved to tears. He clutches my hand during the entire movie. At the end of it, Nick clears his throat. "You scared us shitless. And we don't want to reward bad behavior, as my father would say, but you mean the world to us and we want to make sure you take some time for yourself. So…" He hands him an envelope.

Roberto takes out the piece of paper—a ticket to Italy. "It's a flexi-ticket, so you can use whatever date you want and it's a round-trip, so you do need to come back, but you might be able to go see Giovanni a bit earlier than planned."

Roberto shrieks and jumps and then stops, clutching his side. "I'm supposed to take it easy." He hugs me tightly. "Thank you, thank you, thank you."

The party continues and despite what I said earlier, when Dad doesn't show up, I'm disappointed.

CHAPTER 51 – NICK

TWO WEEKS LATER, the entire show is ready to go. Everyone's talking or thinking or visualizing the movements. I'm in my costume, and I'm so stressed and excited I want to fucking scream. But I don't.

Instead, I glance around and smile when I spot Em. She's talking to Jen. Again. Seeing those two grow closer has been interesting, and seeing Em finding her place has been amazing. She ended up helping with the decorations, but gave up on her dancing spot. Early enough that they could find someone to replace her, and someone who worked her ass off to be the best understudy in history. Jen can't stand that new understudy, but she's trying to stay professional. Jen has definitely left me alone. I apologized to her, but she said she's had her share of mistakes.

Em steps closer to me. She's in a sundress and I don't want anything more than to tug the straps to the side and kiss her neck, her shoulder. But I don't.

"You look nervous. Like, really nervous," she jokes and wraps her hands behind my neck, careful not to touch my makeup. She's no longer a student of the School of Performing Arts after this semester, and I haven't seen her this happy in such a long time, this carefree, this ready to explore the world.

"Me, nervous? Nah. People say to picture everyone in the audience naked, but you know with the lights, I won't see them. And if I do, I'll picture them as zombies eating one another."

"That sounds healthy." She laughs and then squeezes my arm. "You're going to be absolutely amazing. I know it." She pauses. "I have to get back. But *merde*." Her smile widens. "And I love you."

She says it now more easily, but it still means so much to hear those words, and I don't care if Roberto says his sister totally has me whipped. Because she does. And I'm okay with it.

Svetlana enters the room and clears her throat: "This is your moment to shine. Your moment to show your parents, and everyone watching that you are the best of the best, that you're talented and that you love what you do." She gulps. "Some of you will go on to have wonderful careers as dancers. Some of you will maybe decide to dance and then teach. Some of you may want to pursue your training, and some may change their minds." She glances outside the room and winks at Em, who's hiding behind the door. "But tonight, tonight, feel everything. We're proud of you."

And with that pep talk, the buzz intensifies. The director of the School is making a speech on stage, there's a ton of applause and I enter the zone. I'm in the zone. I'm Prince Charming for the evening.

CHAPTER 52 - EM

I'M SITTING IN the front row, next to Nick's mom and dad, next to my family and next to my sister. I glance at the program—Natalya's name should have been there. But Natalya is still in physical therapy, she's still fighting to get back to a level that will allow her to dance professionally. The rumor goes that she might not be able to dance ever again. My throat tightens thinking about how sad she sounded the one time I did get her on the phone.

"Everything is so pretty," Hannah says with awe in her voice and clutches my hand. "Did I tell you Erik wants to have ice cream with me?" She asks with a smile and I grin back. I've met her boyfriend— Erik—last week at the library where he works and he told me he was in love with Hannah. Some people were looking at them sideways when they were holding hands, but their love for one another is one of the most honest I've seen in a long time. Hannah, then,

turns to Mom and talks to her about magic ballerinas and magic Prince Charming.

Mom's been great with Hannah: welcoming and warm. Dad didn't come today—he said he didn't want to intrude, and I think he's giving Mom the space she needs. I'm not sure they'll get back together. I'm not sure she'll ever forgive him for lying to her for so long, for lying to me for so long.

But aside from my dad, it's like for once we're all together to support something bigger than us. And Nick on stage is bigger than us. Much bigger than all of us.

He's leaping and jumping and showing everyone how talented he is. From the corner of my eyes, I see Nick's dad linking his fingers with his wife. "He's good, isn't he?" he whispers, looking at me.

I nod. "He's amazing."

And everyone agrees. The critics. The School. The ballet companies. Everyone agrees that he's the best.

I look at the ceiling, thinking about what Nonna told me. "Nicholas is a good one, Nicholas has a good heart. Listen to yours, Bellisima. Listen to yours."

The back of my throat burns and I blink rapidly, not wanting to become a weeping mess.

Because even though Nonna has been gone for months now, she's still here. She'll always be with me.

ALWAYS SECOND BEST

The next day, I hurry out of the house and almost jog to the metro station. Nick told me to meet him at our spot in Central Park.

When I get there, he's leaning against a tree. He smiles—he's wearing jeans and the shirt I got him that says "Mario Bros. Rocks".

"Hey. Aren't you the new American Ballet Company recruit?" I throw my arms around him. He's been going back and forth between joining a company and changing directions like I did.

He kisses my lips and then my neck and then my lips again. I can feel him smiling. He pulls back a little. "Actually...I'm the new teaching assistant at The School of Performing Arts."

"You are?"

"Svetlana talked to the director and he agreed to give me a try for six months, possibly to be extended for six more months. I get to sleep in the dorms, and I get a meal plan and a very very small allowance. But I don't need help from my parents. I think my dad is actually proud."

I narrow my eyes. "I thought you wanted to dance. Is that what you really want to do?"

"It is. It really is. I'll help teach the freshmen." He pauses. "I have one more year to figure out what I want to do. I love dancing. But for so long, it was something to defy my father with. Something to prove to him. I want to make sure I'm doing it for me too."

He kisses the top of my nose. "Someone smart told me once that I should think about what I want. That I should fight for what I want." His right hand cups my face while the other one trails down my back. And I shiver. "Someone smart once told me I could do

anything I wanted, but that I needed to find something that made me happy." His lips find the spot on my neck that makes my toes curl. "Someone smart once told me that I needed to grow up." His mouth is on mine. A quick peck. "Someone smart once told me…"

"To shut up and kiss me," I reply and pull him to me. This time his mouth isn't tentative, it's demanding and when it opens mine, I press myself further into him, deepening our kiss, deepening our connection. My entire body is in flames and my mind and my heart are burning right along with it. I used to think feeling too much was dangerous. I used to think feeling too much was the best way to get hurt.

But sometimes feeling too much isn't about getting hurt; sometimes it's about putting yourself out there and finding the one who helps you achieve your goals and your dreams. And sometimes that someone just happens to be your brother's best friend.

THE END

A little message to my readers

Dear Reader,

Thank you so much for reading ALWAYS SECOND BEST! I know you have **the** choice between a lot lot loooot of books and I'm grateful you took a chance on mine.
Hope you enjoyed spending **time** with Em & Nick!

Would you like **to read** some **bonus scenes**? Leave an Amazon review for this book and you will receive the **following extra content:**

- Epilogue from Em's point of view
- Epilogue from Nick's point of view

After you leave a review email the link to and I will personally send you the bonus content.

If you want regular updates about my writing, the chance to participate in monthly giveaways and more, you can sign up for my newsletter <u>here.</u>

And, if you're interested in reading exclusive excerpts, a place to hang out and talk books, writing, the ballet dancers who inspired Nick…don't hesitate to join Elodie's Cozy Nook on Facebook.<u>don't hesitate to join Elodie's Cozy Nook on Facebook</u>

Keep on clicking to the end of this book for an exclusive: I'm so happy to share with you the first chapter of NOW & THEN by Jennifer Ellision—keep turning the pages for this little exclusive!

SNEAK PEEK

Do you want to know exactly what happened between Em & Nick last summer? A SUMMER LIKE NO OTHER is !available now!

CHAPTER 1 - EM

The pop music blasts from the speakers so loudly that it resonates within me. I jump once, twice, three times with my fist in the air, and then my hips move to the pounding rhythm.

The mirrors on the wall aren't used to seeing me dance like this. I usually dance to Mozart, Tchaikovsky, Prokofiev, Minkus. Not to Madonna.

I tilt my head to the side. I don't want to rehearse the movements from any ballet choreographies, but I should. I rise on my toes into a *relevé*.

ALWAYS SECOND BEST

I don't want to be Emilia Moretti—sixteen-year-old ballerina who tries to perfect each single movement to the point of obsession. I lower my body down, bending my knees over my feet, into a *plié*.

I don't want to be the girl, who swears she doesn't care about being adopted but who has been trying to find her birth parents.

I stand on my toes again.

I don't want to dwell on the fact that I have the saddest crush on Nick—the best dancer at the School of Performing Arts and my brother's best friend. I want to let go and dance.

I close my eyes and raise my hands, moving my lips and making up words as I sing off-key. I leap from the ground. My legs form a *grand jeté* that would have me thrown out of the School of Performing Arts: my front leg is not entirely straight, and I'm definitely not high enough in the air. But I don't care. I land on one foot, do little jumps and then turn and turn and turn— enjoying the moment, not worrying about anyone possibly watching me.

The summer has emptied the dorms and the hallways of the School of Performing Arts. And if my dad hadn't lost his job, I wouldn't be here either. I would be dipping my toes in the ocean, lying on the beach at the Hamptons, thinking of how to make Nick notice my new bikini. Those days of careless spending and adventures are gone.

My feet take me on another spin. I concentrate on the music, on the feeling of freedom that comes from letting my body move, on the possibilities ahead. Pushing away the thoughts that the music will end, that

I will need to face reality, that this feeling of happiness will disappear.

"Nice, Em. But aren't you supposed to wear clothes when you're dancing?"

I gasp. Nick stands in the middle of the room. Shirtless. His sweatpants hang low like an Abercrombie model's. All strong biceps, ripped abs and chiseled torso.

Note to self: keep breathing.

"Wh-what are you doing here?" I stutter. My heart does its usual happy-to-see-you-Nick dance. Even though, ever since my father got fired, it's been a little tense between us. He's not supposed to be here. He's supposed to enjoy the beach where we used to have bonfires. He's supposed to dip in the water where we played Marco Polo. He's supposed to live the life we used to have. And of course, he's supposed to be tanning on the sand, flirting with every girl in a tiny bikini, breaking hearts.

"Hmmm…what could I be doing in the dance studio?" He raises an eyebrow in his aren't-you-cute-little-sister-of-Roberto way and I want to scream.

But I keep my voice as casual as possible. "Here, in New York." I roll my eyes. Not joining the usual group in the Hamptons may have sucked, but it was supposed to give me at least two months without seeing *him*.

"I was enjoying the show," he replies, laughing

"Yeah. Right." My cheeks flame as I stare into the deep green sea of regrets that is Nick's eyes.

He moves his hips to the music still blasting in the room. A room that is usually able to contain twenty students easily, but which now seems to be closing in on us. "I'm pretty sure this dance is not on the repertoire. But it should be. You looked great and like you were having fun."

"Fun," I blabber. He must be joking: I'm sweaty and out of breath, my hair is probably wild around my face, my posture is all wrong. But he doesn't glance away. His eyes roam my face, down my neck, up and down my body. My almost-naked body. I'm only wearing a bra and tiny shorts. Because I was supposed to be alone here and the stupid AC is being a real diva—working one second and then stopping for a minute while temperatures are hitting the hundreds. My hands curl around my middle, my ears feeling hotter than my own personal Hell.

"You never dance like this—like you're having the best time of your life." His gaze heats up. Or maybe it's me.

My top and my tights sit neatly folded on top of my gym bag. Right by the stereo. I shift on my feet, hesitating. Should I rush to get them? There's something about the way he looks at me that glues me to the floor.

He's looking at me like he sees me. Really *sees* me.

Maybe this is the wake-up call he needed to realize I'm not only Roberto's annoying little sister.

Get a grip, Em. Get a grip.

I clear my throat. "You still didn't answer my question. I thought you were supposed to be at the Hamptons with the rest of the gang." My voice falters but I keep my I-am-not-hurt mask. None of the friends I used to go to the Hamptons with returned my calls. I've received a grand total of one text in the past two weeks, telling me how much fun they're all having and that I'm missing out. Like I didn't know.

Nick crosses his arms over his chest. His very muscular arms. His very defined chest.

I really should get a grip. He's a dancer, he's got an amazing body because he's a dancer, because he puts in a lot of hours into training it, because that's his job. Other guys at the school have a perfect body too. But I don't drool over them, so why him?

He smiles and chuckles. "What's so funny?" I ask, blowing a strand of hair away from my face.

His chuckles turn into one of his happy-laughs, one of his laughs that usually would have me melting. Nick never laughs at me and right now, it almost seems he's trying to push me so I can forget about my bitterness. He winks. "You want to sound angry but you don't. You sound surprised…and maybe, do I dare say it? Happy to see me."

"Yeah, right. You're so full of yourself. Is that a requirement to be one of my brother's friends?" I stretch, grab the remote control lying on the floor and turn off the music. We do not need to have this conversation over the collection of eighties music I found in Mom's closet. Something about listening to "Like a Virgin" right now seems…inadequate.

Or maybe too adequate.

"You know the only requirement to be one of your brother's friends is to like playing *Formula One* and *Mario Kart* and the occasional *Call of Duty*. Your brother is pretty easy to please. You, on the other hand, not so much."

"If my brother is so easy to please, why haven't you been to our place since school ended?" I stare at my shirt as if I could will it to fly to me, as if I developed supernatural powers in the last hour. Going to grab my shirt would mean brushing past him, and I'm not sure my heart could handle the proximity. "I've seen your brother. I kicked his ass at *Formula One* last night," Nick replies.

This time, my smile is real. Roberto hasn't said anything, but he missed hanging out with Nick. I know they only needed a bit of time to figure it out. "I guess I didn't get invited because you were afraid to lose." I can't help but sound a bit smug. I've got mad video-gaming skills.

"Or maybe because you're a sore loser." Nick grins the grin I love, the one that makes my heart beat faster than any ballet rehearsals or showcases.

And apparently, Nick cannot hear the thundering of my heart, cannot hear how it's beating so fast I'm afraid it's suddenly going to stop, cannot hear how it's dancing its own dance for him. Nope, instead of staying at a safe distance, he strides my way, so close I could almost touch him.

This is one of my dreams come true. Dreams. That must be it—I must be dreaming. Which means soon he's going to kiss me. He's going to whisper that he wants me, that's he's always wanted me, that he loves me. I lick my lips and take a deep breath.

But nope, instead of kissing me like he would in my dreams, he smiles one more time, steps away and walks to the bench on the other side of the room. He picks up my clothes, my gym bag and then brings them to me. "Come on, Em. My turn to rehearse."

My stomach clenches and I tilt my chin down.

Definitely not a dream.

Elodie Nowodazkij

And if it is a dream, it's a really shitty one.
A SUMMER LIKE NO OTHER is available now!

ACKNOWLEDGEMENTS

This is my fourth book. My. Fourth. Book. This sounds…amazing.

I wouldn't be publishing my fourth book without the help of my husband, without his support and his love for basil. Maybe one day, we will indeed open this restaurant with a menu only made with basil items. Thank you so much for your support and for your trust in me and my ability to make a career out of my writing. I love you more than cookie ice creams, more than HGTV, more than Mike from *Desperate Housewives* and Debra from *Dexter* combined, more than the food from Favorite and the steak from Delmonico's. You get what I mean. I love you so so so much!!!

This book is in your hands thanks to a lot of people: Riley Edgewood, who not only makes the most wonderful paninis and baked brie (mmm cheese), she is also an amazing critique partner. That scene in the dance studio with the mirrors? You can thank her for that one ☺. Katy Upperman and Alison Miller, who answered and gave me feedback on such a short notice. Plus, their feedback really helped me shape the beginning of this book. Thank you, thank you, thank you! Thanks also to Stephanie Parent for copyediting it, it's so easy to work with you and I feel confident releasing my book after you've worked on making my words all pretty.

This book is also out thanks to all of you who have told me how much you've enjoyed my writing, and Em & Nick especially in *A Summer Like No Other.*

Thank you to the members of my Cozy Nook for your encouraging words, and the chitchat. I love hearing from you and I hope our little Facebook group is a nice place to hang out.

When I'm deep into writing or revising, I sometimes check out on the outside world even though I try not to, but I'm sure it does happen, so thank you to my friends near and far who understand and are there for me.

Every single time I write a book, I tell myself I will make notes of everyone who has played a role, but then I forget. Doh. I really should write in my planner.

This book is about family, and I want to thank my family again. Because, I know how lucky I am. And I miss you all.

Oh, and thanks to my husband's aunt for her name: Svetlana. I hope I used it well ☺

And last but not least, thank YOU. Yes I'm looking at you (well not really, because that would be creepy). Thank you for picking up this little book, for giving me a chance and for giving Em & Nick a chance. I'm crossing my fingers you enjoyed it. Knowing that you've read it is still such an incredible and surreal feeling. I hope I'll never lose that sense of amazement.

<3 <3 <3

About The Author

Elodie Nowodazkij was raised in a tiny village in France, where she could always be found a book in hand. At nineteen, she moved to the US, where she learned she'd never lose her French accent. Now she lives in Maryland with her husband, their dog and their cat.

She's also a serial smiley user.

Visit Elodie online at:
www.elodienowodazkij.com
www.facebook.com/elodienowodazkij
twitter.com/ENowodazkij

EXCLUSIVE FIRST CHAPTER OF JENNIFER ELLISION'S NEW ADULT CONTEMPORARY ROMANCE NOVEL

ONE

EM

Someone smacks me in the face with a hot, wet towel as I walk out the doors of Fort Lauderdale-Hollywood International Airport.

No, wait; that's just the unbelievable Florida humidity.

My feet plod to a halt on the curb with a sigh, scanning the incoming cars for my ride. God, I miss San Francisco already. Had I really crossed the country in an overrated tin can to get here? Had I *really* suffered through seven hours beside a chatty seat mate and a screaming baby for free room and board at Mom's?

I spy a nickel face-down on the ground and nonchalantly toe it until it flips over. Grinning, I palm the dirty coin, reaching into my purse for my wallet. My sad, very empty wallet. I drop the nickel into the coin pocket alongside a wadded up receipt.

My bank account isn't any better. *Tumbleweeds* are more likely to blow through it than a direct deposit.

So, yeah. I'm here for free room and board at Mom's. My job prospects had dwindled in California and my part-time work no longer made ends meet after my roommate moved out. I'd sold or donated pretty much everything I had to get here, refusing to take Mom's money for the ticket. Guilt already twinges at me over finally caving to her wheedling persuasions to come home. I didn't need the weight of a plane ticket added to my shoulders.

I'm just as unemployed here as I'd been out west, but God willing, I'm going to change that before long. Before I start to feel *truly* pathetic.

An obnoxious honking interrupts what promised to be a really stellar pity party.

"Em! *EM*!" My best friend hangs out of her fiancé's car, weaving its way through airport traffic toward me. Nikki waves wildly, corkscrew curls gyrating in the warm breeze.

I'm not ready for this.

Fleetingly, I think of my room back in San Francisco: Quiet. Calm.

And solitary.

I hitch my duffel bag higher on my shoulder and thread my way through cars and people to the dark blue sedan. With her fiancé still at the wheel, Nikki jumps out of the car and pulls me into a tight hug. She stands a full head below me and I rest my chin on her head. It's too almost too hot for the contact, but what the hell? I return the embrace fiercely. It's not as bad in the shade of the airport overpass.

My life back west didn't have many drawbacks, but sometimes, being three timezones away from my friends and family qualified as one of the few.

"Hey, Em." By contrast, Ron's greeting is much more sedate, though he gives me a quick hug and takes my bag to deposit it in the trunk.

"Hey, *Doctor* Ron," I tease, settling into the backseat.

"Still in med school rotations, Em," Ron says, slamming the driver's door shut and easing the car back into traffic. He lefts a genial hand in acknowledgement to the traffic cop who motions us forward. "Not a doctor yet."

"Ignore him. He's brilliant and everyone knows it." Nikki flips a dismissive hand to Ron's modesty and a glint catches the light.

I snatch her hand and yank it toward me.

"Oh, that's right! You hadn't seen it in person yet." She waggles her fingers excitedly in my hand.

"I still won't if you don't hold still."

I'd seen it on Facebook, of course. And in text messages, video chats, Instagrams, blogs— basically if there was a way to document Nikki's path to marital bliss, she'd found it. The ring is pretty. A small, simple solitaire.

Nikki would have been ecstatic over even a baggie tie if Ron had given it to her.

I release her hand. "It's beautiful, Nik."

"Thank you," she trills, straining against the seatbelt to peck Ron on the cheek. He grins and switches lanes.

"I am *so* excited that you're home," she says. "I don't know how I would have planned this wedding without my maid of honor."

"Right. About that." I lace my fingers together and twiddle my thumbs. I'd been dreading this. "I don't know that I'm necessarily the best—"

She swivels in her seat so quickly that she'd give the girl from Poltergeist whiplash. "Emmeline Hayes. Don't you dare tell me that you're not going to be my maid of honor."

"For the sake of everyone in this car, *please* don't tell her that," Ron mutters.

"I am *not* saying that." I emphasize very carefully, lest Nikki attempt to burn me with laser vision. "It's just, I really need to be looking for a job while I'm here."

She still looks like she's trying to kill me with her brain.

"I just mean that I don't see myself having a ton of time to help with wedding plans. Job-hunting, you know?" And I do *not* want to be here until the wedding. They haven't even set a date yet. The idea of wedding planning stretches infinitely forward, with an indeterminate end. Florida is a temporary fix and a temporary fix *only.* I'm here until I can find another job. A job anywhere but here.

"Oh!" Her expression clears. "Don't worry. I have a plan for that."

A plan. Great. A brief history of Nikki's "plans" throughout college flip through my mind like the pages of a book.

And Cole's face is on every. Last. Page.

There's another reason I haven't come home in years. Being here means I'll have to see him again. And the way we'd left things… let's just say I'm not sure what sort of reception I'll receive.

Nikki will notice if I start banging my head against

the window, right?

∞

THEN
Freshman Year

∞

I'd been sleeping fine until the dorm's fire alarm went off with a wail like a banshee.

There was a loud thunk from somewhere in the vicinity of the floor as Nikki fell out of her bed.

"You okay?" I had to shout over the earsplitting sound, pushing my blankets aside. My heart was just beginning to recover from the shock of waking up like that. I shot up, on autopilot, feet already seeking out the pair of sandals I'd left near my bed.

"Fine!" Nikki bolted up, hair standing on end as if she'd been struck by lightning. "Think it's a drill?"

"Don't know." Oh my God, my *ears*. It was like the alarm was prying open my head to ring a gong inside my *brain*.

Nikki tried to stop and check herself for errant

make-up smudges in the vanity mirror, but I shoved her out the door of our room to join the crush of people in the hall. Some, like us, were in their pjs, bed head rampant. Others looked like they hadn't made it to sleep yet. I noted red eyes. Glassy eyes. Sexy-time eyes.

But two of the guys heading from their dorm stood out. Where the rest of us were... well, *dry,* they were soaked from head to toe.

My eyes caught on sodden red hair that bloomed from a short, freckly body. He ran alongside a guy that I would have put money on being his roommate: dripping brown hair hanging into blue eyes that, even from that distance were like ice chips, his face stony. The poor guy's navy t-shirt was soaked, clinging to him like a second skin.

My pulse jumped.

My eyes stayed on him as we ran down the stairs with the rest of the floor. The redhead spouted a continuous stream of apologies, but the brunet boy stayed silent.

"Forget about it. It's fine," he finally said to his roommate. As if the subject of the apology was closed; no longer open for discussion. He crossed his arms over his chest, eyes locked straight ahead, refusing to acknowledge the puddle forming beneath his feet as we stood outside.

God, you could see the muscles right through

his shirt. I stared, transfixed.

"Em? Hellooooo?" Nikki waved a hand in front of my face. I only hoped I hadn't started to drool. She followed the line of my vision.

"Oh, I see," she said with a giggle. "Why don't you go say hi?"

My face heated, trance effectively broken. "No way," I whispered back, mortified to have been caught staring. "What would I say? And keep your voice down. He'll hear you."

"God, I hope so," she said fervently. "Who cares if he hears me? He's cute. You're cute. You could both be cute *together*. Just flirt a little."

"Not a chance in hell."

She bit her lip. I recognized that look in her eyes.

"*No,* Nikki," I said sternly.

She pouted.

"Nikki…"

Before I could stop her, she darted through the mumbling crowd of students who stared up at our building in impatient aggravation. We all wanted to know the same thing: why in God's name we'd been dragged from our beds…

/alcohol…

/studying…

/um… *companions.*

But at the moment, I was far more concerned

with Nikki, who was streaking toward the cute, wet dude like a heat-seeking missile.

There was no way I could have caught her. Tiny Nikki was able to bob and weave through the other students faster than I could ever dream.

"Hi!" She reached him an instant before I did and chirped up at him. "I'm Nikki."

Breathlessly, I stopped short behind her. His eyes zipped to mine and I pulled the sleeves of my sleep shirt over my thumbs.

"This is Em," she continued as though I'd been there the entire time. "Do you guys want to come by our room for dinner tomorrow night?"

I trod on her foot with great precision. To her credit, we'd been friends long enough that this didn't phase her.

Nikki had gotten me as far as an introduction to the cute guy though. At this point, I might as well go all in.

"What she means is 'Hi. Nice to meet you.'" I smiled at them, trying to mask the shred of fading embarrassment that lingered. "And then, I'm *pretty sure* she meant to pause where any normal human would so you could tell us your name before she invited you into our home."

His lips twitched. His eyes lightened up considerably as he lost his stony demeanor. "I'm Cole," he said, extending a hand. "Cole Connors.

Room 311."

"Em Hayes," I said, shaking it. He had a good handshake, I noted. A solid grip; confident, but not intimidating. His blue eyes held me for a minute, like he was measuring me. An unmistakeable arc of electricity jolted through me.

My heart was busy leading a zumba class.

In my throat.

Stop that, I instructed it firmly. This was totally normal. Simple attraction, and nothing more.

"Nikki Wright," Nikki said, enthusiastically pumping his hand when he turned to her next. "Em and I are just down the hall in 309."

"And no pressure," I added lightly. "But if you promise not to tell anyone, I'll let you in on a secret: I *might* be in possession of a hot plate and I don't want to brag or anything, but I make a mean grilled cheese."

He bobbed his head slowly in assent. "That might be cool." Seeming to realize he hadn't introduced the soaking redhead next to him, he indicated the shorter boy. "This is Jerry. My roommate." The roommate in question waved vaguely before shuffling off in the other direction.

Jerry wasn't much for new people, I guessed. Nor did he seem to want to join us for dinner.

"I have to ask," I spoke up. "What's with the wet dog look?"

Cole's eyebrows slammed together and he ran

an agitated hand through his hair. "I don't want to talk about it." But then he seemed to think the better of that statement and it burst out of him in a rush. "No, in all seriousness, it's the stupidest damn thing. My roommate was making pea soup in the microwave."

I raised an eyebrow. "And so then he... threw it on you?" I hazarded a guess.

"I *wish.*"

"Wishing to be covered in hot soup is not a thing most people want." I laughed at the odd phrasing. "You realize that, right?"

Cole hooked his arms behind his neck and rolled it from side to side, the sound of his cracked neck reaching my ears. "He left the room for some reason while it was in there. I had my headphones in, was totally in the zone, and the next thing I know, smoke's pouring out of the microwave. That shit actually caught on *fire.*" His tone was one of disbelief as he shook his head. "Hell of a way to kick off my college career."

"At least it's a night you won't forget," Nikki, ever the optimist, put in.

"Hey, Cole!" A thin, reedy voice interrupted. Cole blinked, looking down near his elbow, where Jerry had suddenly reappeared. "Is it cool with you if I have a couple friends from home over to play video games later tonight?"

Cole blanched. "Jerry, it's three in the morning

already."

Jerry stared up at him expectantly.

"I'm not even sure our electronics are still working after the sprinklers came on."

I'm not even sure Jerry blinked while he waited for an answer.

"Yeah, that's, um…" He sighed, capitulating. "Sure."

He turned his eyes skyward after Jerry darted away.

I wanted to be sympathetic, really I did, but I felt a smile tugging at my lips despite that resolve. Nikki began to giggle openly.

"Okay, look," Cole said exasperatedly. "I don't know anyone here, and this might not be the coolest thing to say to a couple of hot girls that I just met—"

I tried to ignore a jolt of pleased surprise. *He thinks I'm hot.*

"—And I *really* don't want to seem desperate here, but…" He rubbed frustrated hands over his face. "*Help me.*"

It was too much. I couldn't help the laughter that burst out of me.

Cole massaged his temple. "I'm serious," he insisted. "That's my *roommate.* I thought I'd at least have someone that I could hang out with after all of the stupid roommate matching quizzes they made us take, but I'm 99% sure that the only thing we have in common is our non-smoker status. I like video games as much as the next person, but—"

"Excuse me!" A female voice rang authoritatively over the crowd. The buzz of chatter dulled to low murmurs. "Can I have your attention, please!" the woman called, impatience threading its way into her voice.

The murmurs died and silence reigned. "All right everyone," the RA said, standing near the building's turquoise doors. "It's all clear now. It was just a small fire caused by some sort of cooking malfunction—"

Cole covered his eyes with one hand. "Please, God, don't let her say where it started."

"—in room 311."

He sighed. "I hate my life."

"So, everything's safe," the RA continued. "You can all go back to your rooms. And for those of you on the third floor... we're really sorry, but just try to ignore the smell. There's really not much we can do about it."

"There's a smell," Cole stated flatly. He turned to us. *"There's a smell."*

Nikki patted his back sympathetically. "Like I said, we're in room 309. Dinner's at 6:30. See you tomorrow."

Elodie Nowodazkij

ARE YOU AS EXCITED AS I AM ABOUT THIS BOOK? ☺
To know more about it, sign up for Jennifer Ellision's newsletter:

48827652R00182

Made in the USA
Middletown, DE
16 June 2019